DARLING, YOU'VE
CHANGED

Her look se...
behavior was fa...
perhaps, if it we... ...ight
even begin to gi... ...easure . . .

He found her lips. He tenderly kissed her cheekbone before he began a line of kisses moving down her throat.

Wait! What was this upon her skin?

What had happened—

What—

With a cry Rolf sprang to his feet and backed away, almost falling in his haste. Before him now, and lately enfolded most tenderly in his arms was one of the most hideous human shapes it had ever been his ill-fortune to behold. What had been Catherine's healthy young face had altered while he kissed it to the visage of a withered, snaggle-toothed, misshapen crone.

Moving like some crippled sleepwalker, she tottered toward him. "Rolf?" she cawed out the one word, in something like a reptile's voice, and then her figure seemed to blur, and down she fell on hands and knees.

FRED SABERHAGEN

EMPIRE OF THE EAST, BOOK III

ARDNEH'S WORLD

ARDNEH'S WORLD

This is a work of fiction. All the characters and events portrayed in this book are fictional, and any resemblance to real people or incidents is purely coincidental.

Copyright © 1973 by Fred Saberhagen

A Baen Book

Baen Publishing Enterprises
260 Fifth Avenue
New York, N.Y. 10001

First Baen printing, May 1988

ISBN: 0-671-65404-7

Cover art by Greg West

Printed in the United States of America

Distributed by
SIMON & SCHUSTER
1230 Avenue of the Americas
New York, N.Y. 10020

EMPIRE OF THE EAST, BOOK III

ARDNEH'S WORLD

I

Ominor

They were preparing a man for death by slow impalement, for the amusement of the Emperor, who sat in meditative silence amid the blooming drowsy richness of his garden. On the sloping lawn a little below his simple chair, the sharpened stake had been erected in a space framed by formal plantings of tall flowers, among which bees buzzed richly. A few meters beyond that the garden ended at a low sea-wall of stone, and beyond the wall the vast calm lake began. So close was the wall to where the Emperor John Ominor was waiting that with a little effort he might have made a jewel—there was no other kind of stone in easy reach—go splash.

In his view the lake stretched east to meet the sky, and in that sky there frowned a lone high thunderhead, its cloudy base below the watery horizon. Something in the appearance of the cloud suggested a giant air-elemental, but of course that could not really be. The demons charged with the defense of the palace would long since have taken the field against any such intruder, and the sky above the lake would no longer be innocent and summery.

The man who was to die—there was supposedly some evidence to link him with a plot against the Emperor—let out his first unbelieving cry, as the sharpened wood began to have its way with him. Ominor had not been paying close attention, he had larger matters on his mind today, but now he uttered a small sound of satisfaction and leaned back a little in his chair.

The Emperor of all the East appeared to be neither old nor young (though in fact he was very old indeed) and was not noticeably thin or fat. His coloring approximated the human average. His clothes were simply cut, and were for the most part white, with here and there fine trimmings of deep black. Around his neck on a transparent chain there hung a sphere of black, the size of a man's fist, shining as if with oil. It was nowhere pierced by any fastener, but held to the chain by being enclosed in a light basketwork of silver filaments.

While listening to his entertainment, John Ominor gazed out across the near-monotony of the watery plain. Much closer than the thunderhead, but infinitely smaller, a pair of wings were beating, with gradual enlargement. A courier reptile, who perhaps embodied the final relay of a message that had started halfway round the world. This pleasant confirmation of his power crossed the Emperor's mind vaguely; time enough later to discover if the messenger brought good news or bad. His gaze dropped to a fishing boat, that sculled past no more than half a kilometer from shore. His eyes followed a fisherman now, but yet his mind was elsewhere.

Today Ardneh was coming to the palace.

By electronics and witchcraft the Emperor had sought round the whole earth for his most tenacious enemy. At first the objective of the hunt had been simple: to find and kill. Then, when it had become apparent that finding Ardneh's life might be endlessly difficult if not impossible, the searchers' efforts had been bent toward arranging contact, negotiations.

Of enemies John Ominor had plenty, both within and without the power structure he controlled; but Ardneh was unique.

The noises of the impaled man were wholly animal now, and the Emperor turned to watch for a few moments. But he could not relax and enjoy himself, as he had planned to do for a few moments before confronting his visitor. The meeting was now less than an hour away. And Ardneh was beginning to loom too large.

True enough, most of the West looked to Prince Duncan of Islandia as their foremost leader. And Duncan was certainly formidable; he was now maintaining an army on this very continent, where Ardneh's seaboard territory, the Broken Lands and a few other contiguous provinces, gave Duncan a strategic base in which to rest his forces between campaigns. Ominor of course continually planned reoccupation of the seaboard, but somehow could never quite amass enough troops and demons and materiel for the job, not while he was distracted and his strength was drained by a hundred other guerilla conflicts and rebellions around the world. And Duncan would never remain for long in his coastal stronghold, but pour his army out again like some uncontainable liquid into the heart of the continent, where among the vast forests and plains Ominor's generals would fail once again to bring him to decisive battle.

Not far from the sea-wall, and from where the Emperor sat, there stood a summerhouse roofed with dark glass and sided with viny trellises. Glancing toward this shelter, the Emperor saw that his councilors were beginning to assemble within it.

Eight high subordinates had been summoned to attend the confrontation with Ardneh. All wore fine black garments edged and piped with white, negative images of the Emperor's own distinctive garb. When he had counted the six men and two women into the summerhouse, John Ominor rose from his chair and without haste walked down to join them. The two torturers left off their careful work for a moment to fall with foreheads to the ground as he passed near. Ominor glanced with passing amusement at the victim on his stake, boldly upright as if in insolence, and unlikely to be punished for it.

Inside the summerhouse, the eight remained with foreheads against the sandy floor until he had taken the chair at the head of the long table. Then they seated themselves in order of precedence. He was certainly the most ordinary-looking of the nine assembled.

There were no formalities; Ominor simply looked enquiringly at the man who sat at his right hand. This was his chief wizard, the High Sorcerer of all the East, who had many names but was at present known simply and conveniently as Wood.

Wood understood at once what question he was required to answer. He said flatly: "Ardneh is not a human being." Today Wood himself was wearing his most human aspect; he appeared old and gnarled, like some ancient tailor with bowed legs and stringy-muscled arms. He had a big, bent nose, and oddly bulging eyes that very few folk cared to meet.

"Some elemental power, then," the Emperor commented. When confirmation of his statement was not immediately forthcoming, the Emperor added quickly: "Surely Ardneh is not a beast?" Ominor's speech as usual was loud and quick, and as usual it was difficult for his hearers to gauge the exact degree of his impatience.

Wood answered quickly, daring to look his Emperor in the eye. "My Supreme Lord, Ardneh is neither man nor woman, and surely he is no beast. He is therefore a power, but I hesitate to call him elemental. And I think he is not a djinn. He fits no known category. I must confess that there are things about him I do not yet understand."

"An understatement, surely. Keeping in mind this persistent lack of understanding, what do you propose we do today?"

"That we proceed as planned, my Supreme Lord."
The answer came without noticeable hesitation.
Wood could scarcely have maintained his rank just
below the Emperor without considerable courage,
as well as the proper amount of prudence. Around
the table the seven other councilors were waiting,
still as carven images. Abner, High Constable of the
East, commander of Ominor's armies, sat straight
backed at Ominor's left hand, a thick muscle bulging in his neck as he looked with unreadable eyes
past the Emperor at Wood. The Emperor was silent,
watching Wood as he might have watched a prisoner on trial. But it was the way he looked at
everyone.

Wood went on: "If Ardneh is so powerful that we
cannot defend ourselves from him here, at the
center of our world . . ." With a little shrug he let
the sentence trail off.

For a few moments no one in the summerhouse
spoke. From the middle distance came the gurgles
of the wretch who labored hard at dying on his
stake. Then Ominor lifted his weighty gaze from
Wood, and flicked it toward the foot of the table.
"You who labor in the uncommon arts, what can
you tell me today that I have not already heard?"

The junior of the two technologists present only
bowed his head in answer, while the senior stood
up as spokesman, stammering: "V-very little, Supreme Lord. The electronic direction-finding stations continue in operation, and sites for two new
stations have been established since our last meeting. But where the life of Ardneh may be hidden,
that we still cannot say." Candor, even about failures, was the least dangerous course to take with
Ominor. All who survived as his top aides had
learned this well.

Most of the others around the table were indicating by their expressions how scornful they were of
such esoteric methods as the two technologists

were striving to employ. Technology was well enough in its place, making wheels for wagon or chariot, forging swords with hammer, bellows, and anvil. But no one understood electronics, no, not even the technologists who played with Old World gear.

Ominor was not so scornful. The Western enemy had more than once used unorthodox technology with good success.

"Let me hear what the rest of you have to say," the Emperor ordered now, sweeping his eye around the circle. "Can any one of you give me a reason why we should amend or delay our plan for meeting Ardneh?" None could; they murmured one by one, bowed, and shook their heads. The Supreme Lord touched that which hung around his neck, the sphere of blackness on its crystal chain. "And this is what I had best offer Ardneh as a bribe?"

Again the councilors murmured, in a consensus of approval. No one knew exactly what the sphere was, though it was certainly some Old World artifact. Its interior structure, visible only to wizards and quasimaterial, inhuman powers—and presumably to its makers as well—was complex and incredibly beautiful. Demons, djinn, and elementals exposed to the sphere seemed to find it the equivalent of a giant ruby or emerald in human values.

Facing back toward his chief wizard, Ominor returned to an earlier theme: "And what danger will he be to us here, Wood, if he does come?"

"No danger at all, Supreme Lord. My demons and subordinate magicians at every level are alert. Some of the supposedly neutral powers who acted as go-betweens in arranging this meeting are—as you know, Supreme Lord, but some of your councilors may not—secretly in our service. Ardneh has been too distrustful of them to let them find out much about him, but they report no indication that he is planning any attack on us today. Would that he did attempt to strike at us! To do that he would have to gather his full presence here, not only, so to speak, send us his eyes and ears and voice and little more. The more powerful his manifestation, the more he will render himself vulnerable. My demons are ready, their jaws will close upon him." Behind the wizard Wood, above the innocent lake, the air shimmered for a moment, and there were visible in it three pools of shadow, distinct for a moment despite the sun. Then the air steadied, and all was azure summer once again. Wood went on: "I earnestly desire that he will try to attack us here today, but I fear he is too clever."

But Ominor did not seem satisfied. His manner was that of a probing judge. "Our potential visitor, whom you say your powers are set to spring upon, slew the great demon Zapranoth, in the Black Mountains, as easily as a man might crush a toad. So you have reported to me."

Wood blinked, and then it almost seemed he smiled. "Zapranoth of the Black Mountains, Lord? Yes. But do not attach too much importance to that. To the least of these three powers in the air behind me now—to the least of them, Zapranoth was vassal. Of demons greater than these three above the lake there is only—one." Wood's voice dropped on the last word, but still it seemed to have a special emphasis.

The plan for a direct confrontation with Ardneh had been Ominor's own idea. A month ago he had broached it to his council arguing thusly: The power called Ardneh was certainly a sore annoyance to the East, though (as yet, at least) he could not be considered a mortal threat. Ardneh seemed to seldom or never appear in his own form, if he had one. Instead he worked in one human avatar after another, subtly possessing or influencing men to his own ends, which seemed to be in general agreement with those of the West, though

Western wizards were thought not to have any certain control over Ardneh. Usually Ardneh worked so smoothly and carefully that his chosen host or partner seemed to feel that he was acting on his own. Only the greatest wizards on both sides of the war, and the high leaders they advised, were fully aware of how much the recent successes of the West were due to Ardneh.

Growing impatient of managing any direct attack upon this subtle foe, Ominor had settled on subversion, laced with treachery, as a logical alternative.

Now in the garden the cries of the impaled man were weakening rapidly. The torturers had prudently withdrawn a little distance, to be well out of earshot of the conference in the summerhouse, and as a consequence the victim seemed likely to enjoy a relatively rapid death.

Ominor, as the executioners had judged, was paying no further attention to the diversion. Having completed his brooding, almost accusatory survey of his aides, he got to his feet and said: "Then let us bring him. On with it."

The conference broke up. The lieutenants of the powerful councilors hastened to them to receive orders. Soon all the garden back to the ivied palace wall was cleared of common soldiers, slaves, and everyone else not concerned directly with the coming confrontation. The torturers before they left were told by Wood that they might let their victim stay, told by Wood who nodded to himself as he spoke and thought that he saw opportunity here.

Explaining his thought to his Lord of Lords, the wizard said: "Ardneh has in the past once or twice possessed such a victim and acted through him. We shall have him, if he dares to try that trick today."

Ominor thought briefly, then nodded his agreement. Followed now by a deferential train, he left the summerhouse and moved a short distance to where Wood's assistants were beginning to set the stage for the encounter. This was on a flat paved

place some ten meters square, bordered on one side
by the low balustrade that guarded the sea wall's
outer edge, the lake rippling and chuckling some
four or five meters below. The Emperor beheld several of Wood's most able aides, master wizards
themselves in any company but his, on their knees
on the pavement, with chalk and charcoal making
most careful diagrams.

Now the word was sent at once through inter-
mediary powers to Ardneh that he was expected,
under truce, as soon as he could manifest himself.

Some time passed. "What is going on in the mind
of our guest?" the Emperor asked, breaking a little
silence that had fallen on the group. "Is he having
second thoughts about the wisdom of paying us a
call?"

Wood lifted his gnarly hands, let them dangle in
front of him as if seeking to dry them in the breeze.
His two little fingers moved slightly, twitching like
insects' antennae. "Supreme Lord, he is near."
Wood's bulging eyes, looking blind now, seeing
more than any other eyes present, gazed out across
the lake, "My Emperor, he is approaching. When
you can see something near at hand above the water, speak and he will hear."

Ominor at first saw only the distant fishing craft,
and the towering cloud unchanged. Then, following
a subtle gesture from Wood, he brought his attention closer to the shore, and noticed a patch of
ripples somehow different from all the rest. At any
other time he would probably have taken them for
some effect of wind. But steadily they came closer,
not blending like other waves into the general motions of the water. The Emperor was magician
enough to feel it now. A hint of arrogant immensity.
The presence of hostile power, aloof, quiet, waiting.
The ripples, slowing their progress gradually,
drifted to within a dozen meters of the low balustrade. Ominor's accustomed eyes could tell now
that above the ripples there was — something.

In his loud voice filled with certitude he said: "Hear me, dullard of the West! It must be plain by now, even to you, that the hour of your complete destruction cannot be far away. Yet I admit that it lies in your power to cause me some inconvenience still. And rather than see such abilities as you possess turned into nothingness, I would bring them into my domain. I am willing that you should receive some substantial rank in the hierarchy of the East, one that is probably higher than you dare to expect."

He had spoken slowly enough for his hearer to have readily interrupted him with an answer at any of the several places. But there was no answer. The Emperor glanced at Wood and at his other waiting councilors, but got no help. Whether Ardneh's silence was born of an attempt to impress them, or of fear, or of some other cause, there was no clue.

Under these conditions Ominor had no intention of going on with a long-winded speech. At the moment he had only one more thing to say: "In token of my sincerity . . ." And pulling from around his neck the crystal chain with its impressive burden, he whirled it once around his head and sent it flying out over the water, spinning in the sun. He watched for the bribe to vanish, into seeming air or in the grasp of some materialization. But the Emperor was disappointed; the treasure only splashed and sank, prosaically as a lump of rock, going quickly out of sight in the deep water.

Where no more strange ripples moved. The air was empty once again.

Close by his side, Wood said: "Supreme Lord, the creature is gone. All contact has been broken."

The Emperor felt his tension slide away. Through him in a flash there passed understanding, contempt for his enemy, and elation. "He did not take the prize."

"No. It lies somewhere in the water there."

The Emperor jutted out his chin, his teeth bared

in a smile. That Ardneh might take the bribe and then refuse to honor it had been considered; it would have meant no serious loss. Of course it had been expected that he might refuse with some contemptuous speech or gesture. But to cut and run, in panic . . . it could scarcely be anything else. The quasimaterial powers were if anything more concerned than humans were with saving face. Overawed by the Emperor and his wizards, frightened by the palace guard of monstrous demons . . .

Suddenly suspicious, Ominor asked Wood: "Do you suppose he smelled the poisoned bait?" The ebon sphere had been laden with the most subtle and powerful curses Wood could devise.

"Nay, great Lord." Wood too was smiling in this moment of success, having proven his ability to control the greatest of enemies at close quarters.

Turning away from the balustrade, the Emperor walked deliberately back in the direction of his palace, massed behind its palisade of trees.

Without turning or pausing, the Emperor ordered Wood: "Make some suitable plan to rid us of this creature Ardneh. We know now he can be no mortal threat. Still . . ."

"Yes, Lord of Lords." Turning momentarily to a subordinate, Wood said in an aside: "Use great care in recovering the poison bauble from the water. Better set a guard, and let it lie awhile. Who so comes into possession of it in the next hour will need all my skill to keep him healthy."

The Emperor's train moved on at an easy pace toward the interior of the palace grounds. There was a feeling of general relief in the air. Ordinary servants were beginning to reappear, soft gongs were striking a time-signal for mid-afternoon. Between beds of unusually luxuriant flowers Ominor paused, and the lawn chair he had been sitting in earlier was instantly unfolded and placed ready for him.

There were several business matters to be attended to. All were comparatively minor things, however, and within half an hour the Emperor was signing the last required paper, with relief because he felt inexplicably tired. Raising his eyes, he saw coming from the central parts of the palace an oddly mixed group of about half a dozen men. A pair of them were high-ranking wizards, two at least were household stewards, some were members of his personal bodyguard. All were moving with a sort of reluctant haste toward John Ominor, as if none of them wanted either to be first with whatever news they bore, or to give any appearance of delay.

He stood up and his legs nearly failed him. In his guts there twisted something like the leaden claw of death. Another poisoning plot uncovered, then. Perhaps too late, this time. Wood came from somewhere, maybe out of the air, to stand before him gesturing, and the pangs in his midsection began to ease, reluctantly.

And now Ominor saw what those coming from the center of the palace were holding up on its crystal chain. He heard their disjointed, fearful explanations of how it had just been cut from the belly of a huge, fresh-caught fish, one marked for the Emperor's dinner.

Wood's chief assistants were coming running to join him, to help to combat the deadly spells they had so recently set in motion. As soon as he felt a little better, Ominor called to him the High Constable, Abner.

The soldier towered above his chair. "My Emperor?"

"The wizards have failed me. There is a mission I want you to undertake. We must learn, begin to learn, what Ardneh is."

II

Summonings

———————◆·◆◆·◆———————

In Rolf's dream the demon uttered a deafening warcry and slew the world, cutting the life from it with one sweep of a great two-handed blade. The blade drew with it the blackness of oblivion, drew a curving black wall that completed itself to make a sphere and put an end to all light everywhere. Rolf cried out in fear, and leaped backwards to save himself, knowing that to save himself was what he had to do to save the world.

Before he was fully awake he was on his feet, starting up with sword in hand from where he had been lying cloak-wrapped in the long grass, stretched out sleeping on soft earth. Dazedly he realized that his outcry had not been confined to the world of dreams; his nine comrades in the patrol had been awakened, were gathering with hasty caution round him in the dark; and others elsewhere might have heard the yell also.

"I dreamed, I dreamed, I dreamed," he kept on whispering, till he was sure the other soldiers understood. They muttered and grumbled and listened in the night, for the approach of some alerted enemy.

At last, amid some sour, whispered jokes, Mewick, the patrol commander, ordered as a precaution that all should mount; they were to move camp by a kilometer or so. This was quickly accomplished, for here on this vast, grassy plain one spot was much like another, and there were no tents and little baggage. Then with the camp re-established, riding-beasts once more picketed and a pair of sentries posted, Mewick came to where Rolf was sitting and squatted down beside him.

Neither spoke for a while. It was a warm and moonless night, with a thick powdering of stars showing irregularly between smooth-flowing, barely visible clouds. The insects of early summer racketed in the tall grass.

After a few moments Rolf whispered: "It was a warning, I believe."

"Of what?" Mewick's voice was soft, as usual. "Shall I call Loford here?"

"I can talk to him now, or in the morning. But there is little I can tell him." Already the dream was disintegrating in the grip of clumsy waking memory. "There was danger, and a sense that I must act at once, to save myself. Not just fear, but a sense that my life was—valuable."

Mewick nodded, considering. "Talk to Loford in the morning, then. But are you going to jump up yelling again the next time you go to sleep?"

"Sleep seems far from me now," Rolf said. "I'll take a turn at sentry-go."

"No. You stood your watch. Sleep now. The dawn is not far away."

Rolf shrugged, and stretched out on the ground, pulling his cloak round him, making sure that his weapons were in easy reach. He closed his eyes, though he felt sure that he was not going to get any more sleep . . .

. . . and this time the demon-monster's sword was coming right at *him*, with body-splitting force. His leap and yell were no more under voluntary control than the gush of blood from a new wound. His waking convulsion left Rolf on his feet with sword in hand once more, knowing that once more he had put his comrades all in danger . . .

An Eastern soldier, real and solid as the grass and earth, was crouching just three meters off, sword half raised for the easy stroke that would have drained Rolf's sleeping life into the soil. A dim, tense outline in the deceptive, grayish predawn light, the man got his blade up in the way of the hard over-hand cut Rolf aimed at him. But the parry was not made with sufficient force, and the man's face and shoulder erupted blood. He grunted, and could do nothing else before the next blow came to kill him.

The others of what happened to be an exception-ally competent Western patrol were springing up at hair-trigger tension from what could have been no more than light, uncertain sleep. Tall Chup hewed right and left and the Eastern men he struck fell back like children knocked aside. And Mewick seemed to be fighting on both sides of Rolf at once, opponents toppling before his battle-hatchet and short sword as if it were a dance they had rehearsed. And years of hard experience had made Rolf a better fighter than most. As soon as he had finished his first opponent, he turned with methodical swift-ness to find another.

A white flash came inside his skull, a painless, noiseless, stunning blast. With a moment of intense clarity of thought he knew that he was wounded, and waited with a certain detachment to find out if he was slain. He felt no agony, no sickening shock, but still his legs betrayed him and he fell.

Ardneh. The half-familiar, subtle and inhuman presence was with him suddenly and reassuringly, more powerfully and personally than ever before, unmistakably the same as that which had brushed him when he rode the Elephant.

Ardneh, he thought, do not make me fall, help me to rise. But down he went, to lie on his face in the deep grass while struggling feet ripped through it all around him. Rolf could not move, but his mind was clear, and knowledge was sent him from a voice-less and unseen source. It was Ardneh himself who had wakened him with warning dreams, to keep him from being slaughtered in his sleep, and Ardneh also who had just struck Rolf down. He was being

kept out of the fighting, for some purpose he could
not yet plainly see.

Something that was of awesome, overriding importance . . . but right now his field of vision was
cut to a one-eyed view of grasstalks, and his own left
hand. He could feel that his right hand still held his
sword, but it was not by any conscious management
of his.

The fighting and chasing around him seemed to
go on endlessly. Time was slow at the bottom of the
tall grass. He was given reassurance, in Ardneh's
subtle, wordless way, that the West was winning the
skirmish. Ardneh had many other demands upon
his energy. Rolf was going to be left to himself now to
recover, which should not take him long.

An age or two had passed before he heard the
voices of some of his friends, dourly cautious, com-
menting as they found the body of one of their sentries, slain by stealth. The other sentry had come
through all right, it seemed, as had the animals.
Now feet trampled close to Rolf again, surrounded
him, and stopped.

Mewick's soft voice announced it simply: "Rolf is
dead."

Hands turned him over; when his living face appeared under the now-brightening sky, voices ex-
claimed in surprise.

Rapidly, now that he had been moved, the life
flowed back into his limbs. He sat up, breaking out
in a cold sweat. To a flurry of questions, he
answered with such explanation as he could give.
He did not understand it very well himself.

Loford, who was the only wizard present, listened
with grave headshakings and then conferred with
Mewick. Then Loford drew from his bag of magical
apparatus a thin slab of wood in two parts, hinged
like a folding game board. Loford cleared a little flat
space on the ground and put down his board, and
on it he cast straws once, twice, thrice, to see in
which direction the patrol should move next. No

divination was infalliable, of course, but Mewick wanted all the help he could get in reaching a decision.

With each cast the indicated direction was the same. Northwest. Mewick, watching closely, wore a deeper frown than usual. There was, or should be, little that way but unpopulated wasteland for a thousand kilometers or more.

In response to an inquiring look from his commander, Loford said succinctly: "Ardneh." Then he murmured the words of the appropriate spell and tried again.

Northwest.

"North." The word came firmly, in the voice of the young seeress, Anita, whose advice was so often hesitant. Prince Duncan of the Offshore Islands, who had been leaning forward in expectation of a struggle to catch some mumbled obscurity, eased back now in his camp chair. Here, many kilometers west of Mewick's patrol, the dawn was yet no more than a faint promise, and a lamp was lit inside his tent.

The girl Anita, mumbler though she usually was, had been proven the most reliable oracle that Duncan had yet been able to conscript. With Duncan's chief wizard Gray now standing at her shoulder, she sat in a chair opposite Duncan's, her breathing deep and slow and her eyes fixed somewhere over the Western commander's shoulder.

"Anita." Duncan's voice was insistently reasonable. "Why should we march into the north?" The map of the continent, spread out in his mind's eye, could give no reason, except possibly to confuse the enemy. Nothing lay to his north but a thousand kilometers of wasteland. To Duncan it seemed likely that some enemy power was working through the seeress now despite Gray's precautions, trying to lead them into a trap.

Anita answered: "To win the war. More I must not

tell you at this time." The voice was the girl's own, which was unusual for one possessed by a power; and this sudden cool assumption of authority was startling, whoever the power might be.

Duncan's head lifted. "Are you Ardneh?" he asked sharply.

"I am," said the girl, looking at him with an empress' manner. When herself, she was too shy to meet his eyes for long.

Behind the girl's chair, tall Gray turned startled eyes to meet Duncan's, then slowly nodded: in his opinion it was Ardneh. For the moment Duncan could say nothing. Ardneh had never made contact with him before, but Duncan had pondered long, trying to decide what course he should take when the meeting did take place, as seemed inevitable. He had come to no decision, but now he must; what attitude should he—and, in effect, the entire human West—take with regard to the being who called himself Ardneh?

It was very quiet inside the tent. The army lay, to protect it against discovery by spying reptiles during the day, within a forest of high-crowned trees. Duncan could now hear the small creatures that dwelt in the branches above his tent, beginning their stirrings of the day.

Ardneh was unique. No wizard of West or East could understand him. He was subtle, but the power . . . In the struggle with Zapranoth, the very mountains had been cracked. That much Duncan had seen for himself, afterward. It was as if the obscure Old World quotation were true indeed, that some put into Ardneh's mouth: *I am Ardneh, who rides the Elephant, who wields the lightning, who rends fortifications as the rushing passage of time consumes cheap cloth . . .*

But could the West take this unidentified power as unquestioned leader, king and Lord?

Duncan arose and moved to the doorway of his tent, a moderately tall young man with sunbleached

long hair and a face that worry and weather had
made look older than it was. Moving outside, he
ignored, because he was not conscious of it, the
salute of the runner waiting before his tent, who
sprang up ready for duty. The camp, almost soundless and invisible in the pre-dawn dark, stretched
unseen before Duncan.

Now, on Ardneh's unexplained—wish, order,
whatever you wanted to call it—he was supposed to
swing his whole army north, a move for which there
seemed to be no military justification. No, there
could be no thought of making such a move on trust.

Duncan spun and re-entered the tent. Facing the
girl who was still in trance, he snapped: "What will
happen if I do not move the army as you say?"

Without hesitation Anita replied: "You will lose
the war."

"How am I to know that you are to be trusted?"

"By its fruit the tree is known."

Duncan grunted. He thought a moment more,
then barked orders to his wizards, directing them to
prepare alternate means of divination. He watched
while they roused the girl from trance, and remembered to say a kind word to her as she was taken out,
flustered, shy, and unremembering. Then he called
for and quickly ate a hearty breakfast, meanwhile
hearing reports brought in by birds just in from
their night's scouting.

The daylight was not yet full when Duncan left his
tent again to stride out through the sprawling camp.
He passed among rows of quiet tents, and of men
and women sleeping cloak-wrapped on the earth.
Some were up and about, readying food for the
morning meal, repairing gear, cleaning, washing,
inventorying, sharing out supplies. Up in the trees,
if you looked for them, the returned birds were visible, brownish gray and shapeless, hiding heads and
eyes against the glare of day.

Now the rows of tents were left behind. Passing a
sentry who informally nodded to him in recogni-

tion, Duncan entered denser forest. Soon he had
reached gloomy thickets through which the eye
could scarcely find a pathway. But now as Duncan
continued to step forward one bush or another bent
itself aside for him. he kept unhesitatingly to the
path thus indicated. He had come some fifty paces
past the last human sentry before he got a direct
look at his pathmaker: a forest elemental, almost
tree-like in appearance, raised great gnarled limbs
at some distance to Duncan's left. It was guiding
him in turns and doublings, supposedly preventing
the approach of any unfriendly power.

At length the parting of a final screen of bushes
disclosed before him a wide, still glade. In the middle of the glade there stood three men, or at any rate
three tall forms, seemingly garbed more in darkness
and in light than in any human-woven cloth. They
were his three chief wizards, Duncan knew, but
which of them was which he could not have
guessed. The three turned simultaneously to face
the Prince as he stepped out of the bush.

He could not see their faces clearly and did not
try. As had been prearranged, in a loud voice he
demanded: "Ardneh, Ardneh, Ardneh! Who is he?
What is he? Will it be to my advantage to trust his
word, to heed his will, to follow where he leads?"

One magician threw back his head, cowled and
faceless, and replied: "If we do not trust and heed
and follow him, I see the end of the war."

"That has a hopeful sound."

"The end of war, the backs of Western men bent
hopelessly under the Eastern lash, their babies
slain, their women and their lands despoiled. That
is the future I see if we reject the power called
Ardneh now." The faceless speaker bowed his head.

A second spoke: "Lord Duncan, if we do trust the
power called Ardneh now, I see no swift end to the
war. I cannot see an end at all."

"Bah! All things in this world have an end. Still,

better an augury of uncertainty than one of doom.
What else?''

The second wizard continued: "I see that fearful
things must fall upon our people, if we heed the call
that Ardneh sends today.''

He who had spoken first to Duncan raised his
head again at that, and said: "You do not tell what all
of us must see, that fearful things must fall upon us,
soon, whatever the good Prince chooses.''

Duncan put in, impatiently: "It is war, and we all
know what that short word means. Can you add to it
aught of fear that we have yet to learn?''

And the second seer: "This much; I see
Ardneh—not clearly, but I know that it is he—
caught in the grip of some power of evil stronger
than he is, caught and dying whilst our army flees
from trying to help. This the result if we listen to him
now, accept his leadership. If we do not, I cannot
see his death, or even the appearance of this enemy
of incredible strength.''

The two magicians who had so far spoken fell
silent now, looking at Duncan, then turning to follow the direction of his eyes with their own.

The third wizard, who seemed now to stand the
tallest, broke his silence. "Lord Duncan, it is all true,
what both of them have told you. If we accept the
leadership of Ardneh, I see Ardneh ringed about
with enemies and dying, and I see you despairing in
retreat. And then . . . that vision ends in some great
violence. If we do not accept and follow Ardneh, the
vision is even clearer, and, at least to me, even more
terrible. For in it the West and all it stands for is no
more . . . ''

"Hold!'' Duncan commanded. "All of you! If by
your arts you can see these things, must not Ardneh
be able to see them too?''

The three conferred together, whispering. Then
the first replied: "It would seem to be not beyond
his powers.''

"Well, then, if he is truly on our side . . ." Duncan lost the thread of what he had meant to say. Perhaps he was distracted by the way the three faceless wizards were now all turned toward him with a certain new tension in their postures, as if they had suddenly seen something new and peculiar about him.

It occurred to him also that he should take more time to think about the patrols he had routinely scattered in all directions to see what . . . no, especially he must consider those working far to the north and . . . actually, one patrol in particular required some thought. One of the men in it was a black-haired youth, short but strong-looking, named Rolf or something like that. Yes, perhaps he had heard of this Rolf before—some matter connected with technology. Ardneh might well now want this Rolf to do something technological again, since whatever it was before had worked out so well.

As Duncan thought further he seemed to see deeper into the matter. It came to him, as a remembered secret that should be shared with few or none, that this new technological mission for which Rolf (and the patrol that included Rolf) should be diverted would probably involve a certain object black as shiny ebony, a somehow gem-like thing about the same size as a man's clenched fist. Ardneh had probably handled a similar thing recently, seen and handled such a thing for the first time, and in the course of that handling had obtained a clue as to the existence and whereabouts of this larger and vastly more valuable one, the true worth of which was not yet appreciated by any human being. It was now in the possession of some adherent of the East, somewhere in a northern desert where the patrol of which Rolf was a member, if they were fast enough and lucky enough, might be in time to intercept . . .

So smoothly and with such seeming rightness did this train of thought flow through Prince Duncan's mind, that only after it had progressed thus far did he awake to the fact that it was bringing him new knowledge, that it must have its origin in some mind other than his own.

Ardneh? he demanded, silently, but with a concentrated urgency of thought that was the equivalent of a shout. There was no answer, save that the flow of ideas about the gem-like thing, whose existence he had never before suspected, broke off.

Ardneh, you cannot manage me that way. I will not be controlled. But even as his challenging thought went forth he knew that no effort had been made to control him. He had only been taken partly into Ardneh's confidence.

The air within the glade had cleared. The wizards once again had faces, and were pressing round him anxiously. " . . . Lord Duncan, Prince," tall Gray was repeatedly demanding. When he saw that Duncan was aware of him, he added: "He came to you directly. Prince, did you not feel his weight?"

"Yes, yes. Now I have felt him. Listened to him. Whether I believe him is still another question."

They pressed him for more information but there was little more that he could tell; Ardneh was still a mystery. He led the others back to the camp, where he plunged alone into his tent for a time to argue with himself amid maps, reports, intelligence estimates. There were strong arguments on both sides, but already in his heart he was more than half convinced that soon he would be moving the army north.

III

Banditry

———◆◆◆———

Full summer had come, and Abner, High Constable of the East, with the dust of hard journeying upon his clothes, sweltered standing in the small room high under the sun-beaten roof of the caravanserai. Around him a few quick and silent servants hurried, nimbly adjusting their movements in the cramped quarters to the Constable's bulky, careless presence. Dust raised by hasty efforts at cleaning still hung visible before the small, high windows in the prison-like walls. The servants were unpacking things and moving the Constable in with practiced efficiency, while he looked around him with distaste. The place had looked more inviting from the outside. It would have been better, the Constable was thinking now, to have camped in the open again; his escort was strong enough to have nothing to fear from bandits, and there could be no sizable Western force in the area. But his companion had wanted to spend a night or two indoors, and to humor her he had agreed.

Of course he could change his orders and move out again, but he had had a weary day in the saddle and was not minded to wait longer for his bath and such pleasures as the evening might afford. So let it be. In the next room of his little suite, which was of course the least dilapidated of the establishment, he could hear the buckets of bath-water already being carried in. Standing by a window and tall enough to peer down from it, he could see in the courtyard below how the weary loadbeasts of his retinue were being unloaded, watered, and bedded for the night.

The south wall of the courtyard below was pierced by a single central gate, the only way in or out. On the other three sides were buildings, all the same three-story height. The building the Constable stood in, and the one opposite, were divided into small apartments and barrack-like chambers, the ground floors usable interchangeably by animals or by humans of the lower classes. The building that formed the third side of the enclosure, opposite the gate, contained a tavern, a brothel, a store, and the small quarters of the Master of the Station and his few permanent guards. All the buildings had windows only on their inner sides, facing the central square, and in their outer walls mere arrow-slits.

Probably a couple of hundred people were now inside the walls, two-thirds of them in the Constable's retinue. Nor had they seen another living human during the last two days. This remote region of the continent seemed to have been forsaken even by the war. Here and there moved roving bands of outcasts, deserters from East and West. But as for Duncan, his maneuverings, like Ominor's, were many kilometers to the south.

The Emperor of the East had assumed command of his own armies in the field, freeing his Constable for another mission, that of learning about Ardneh. The magicians had failed miserably. Abner had the Emperor's trust, as much as anyone could be said to have it. He was journeying widely in this desolate part of the country to interview people, mostly Eastern officers, who in the past in one way or another had had something to do with Ardneh. More such Eastern people were to be found here than anywhere else, because those who had survived a struggle with Ardneh-inspired forces tended to be under a cloud of failure, and those whose failures were deemed mild tended to be assigned to remote places where nothing important depended on them. Those whose failures were thought grave by Ominor were seldom in any condition to be interviewed.

Of course Abner might have summoned to the capital the people he wanted to talk to, eyewitnesses who had been engaged in the various battles in which Ardneh was known to have taken a hand. But then they would keep re-working their stories to put themselves in a more favorable light. He had to convince them that information was what he wanted, not more scapegoats. Just talking directly to the High Constable was intimidating enough for most of them.

A few had other reactions. One of these had engaged the Constable's interest for reasons that had nothing to do with Ardneh; she had been traveling with him now for half a month. Two days after he met her he had sent home his other concubines.

The stone walls of the caravanserai were thick, but the fit of the massive wooden doors was far from tight, and now from the apartment next to Abner's there came plainly the slide and thump of baggage being moved, and the voice of the Lady Charmian in the shrill tones she used with servants. Abner listened. In the very ugliness of that voice, which at other times could hold all the female sweetness in the world, there was a fascination. Even by its incongruity the voice evoked the unbelievable beauty of her face and body. Truly a most remarkable woman, even in the eyes of a man who had his pick of what the East and the subjugated lands could offer. And it was a nice touch that he could blend his business with his pleasure. Charmian had been at the debacle of the Black Mountains. Not that she had been able to tell him much of Ardneh.

Abner squinted against the lowering summer sun in the northwestern sky. Along the shaded porch of the brothel-tavern, some of its girls were quarreling,

and had reached the stage of pulling hair. At the
other side of the courtyard, three travellers, evidently some kind of traders, were being let in
through the massive, narrow gate.

. . . yes, the woman was already assuming a
ridiculous importance in his life. Not for the first
time, he suspected magic. When he heard the door
close behind his servants and knew he was alone he
reached for amulets of great power that hung
around his neck inside his outer garments. With
these devices given him by Wood himself, Abner
probed for any indication of a love-charm being
worked. But to his passes and mutterings now no
answer came. The woman's magic was no more than
feminine beauty and cleverness. No more? Those
were quite enough.

When Abner had met Charmian she was living
with the commander of a small cavalry post, in a
place even more desolate and isolated than this
caravanserai—a great come-down for her. Obviously she saw Abner as a miraculous chance to not
only regain lost ground but leap far ahead of the
places she had fallen from. The lady wanted power
and position, and would spare no pains to get them.
The cavalry commander had been unable to hide his
chagrin at his loss, when Abner had invited the lady
to accompany him, even as she herself had been
openly overjoyed. Well, someday Ominor might
claim her for himself; but neither he nor Abner
would ever be so openly dismayed at the loss of this
or any other woman . . .

Rolf, Chup, and Loford, having passed the brief
scrutiny of the Master of the Station and been admitted through the gate—no very strict precautions
against bandits were being taken, it seemed, because of the unusually large party of armed men
who lay within the walls tonight—were sent on to
find such lodgings as they might. They had put on

clothing suitable for merchants and had counter-
feited the general appearance of such as well as they
were able. Their apparent caste thus achieved
might at another time have gained them lodgings in
the second or possibly the uppermost floor of one of
the dormitory buildings, but today a small room on
the lower level of servants and stables was the best
that they could do. The Constable's retinue and a
party of well-to-do slave dealers had taken over everything else from the top down.

Even with some guidance from Ardneh it had
taken Mewick and his patrol several weeks to find
Abner's trail. They had been following him closely
for four days now, being too few to attempt an open
assault on such a large party. Rolf still felt the certainty, send wordlessly by Ardneh, that the strange
object they were to seize was in the baggage of
Abner or someone traveling with him. Ardneh's in-
fluence had become so convincing that Mewick had
turned his patrol in the desired direction even before orders to do so came by bird-messenger from
Duncan. The orders when they came were explicit,
brought by birds who told how Duncan was starting
to turn his whole army north: the seizure of the
jewel was to be attempted at all costs to the patrol.

Abner's decision to stop at the caravanserai offered at least some prospect of a chance. Thus, the
plan to send three men behind the same walls as the
Constable. The very added security of the walls
might induce the enemy to let down his guard, and
make some action possible.

Once in their ground-floor room, which they had
claimed by evicting a miscellany of beasts of burden
into the open courtyard, the three putative merchants had no difficulty, looking out through their
uncloseable window, in picking out the high narrow
windows of the Constable's chambers in the building opposite. It was certain that he would have
taken the poor best that the place could offer; and
Chup and Loford had had enough experience with

caravanserais of similar design to know where the most desirable rooms must be.

After seeing to their animals, and stowing their meager baggage in the most easily watched corner of their room, the three of them held converse in voices inaudible more than an arm's length away.

Chup mused: "It will not be easy, I think, to get near enough to strike."

Loford could look the mild tradesman part quite easily, and had been the spokesman at the gate. He answered now: "It is too early yet to tell. Give them a night of carousing, and see if by tomorrow they have not begun to be a little slow to notice things, a little lazy."

Rolf said: "Also, remember this. Just getting near and striking will not avail us anything."

Chup shook his head a centimeter or two in disagreement. "To kill Abner would be something, a deep wound for the East. Worth taking a chance for, whether or not we can do the job for which we came."

Rolf, putting flat authority into his quiet voice, said: "No, to kill Abner is nothing if we cannot get the stone we want and get away with it. So Ardneh says." Beyond that he could give his friends no explanation, for Ardneh had given none to him. Should Rolf be captured and questioned, still he would be able to say no more. But he spoke with conviction, having faith in Ardneh.

The other two exchanged a look of age and experience above his head. "Well," said Chup, "what you say about getting away is suitable to me. I have no objection to my own survival.'

Loford put in: "Suitable, and interesting. Sometimes it pays to plan from start and finish toward the middle. Suppose we have what we came for, and are getting away—will we absolutely need the animals that we rode in here on?"

"No," said Rolf. "Mewick and I discussed that. There are at least three good spare animals with the patrol. If we can rendezvous with them outside the walls all should be well."

"And I," said Chup, "came thinking we might go out over the roof." He patted his midsection under his loose merchant's garb. "I have some rope coiled here. That gate seems to be well watched, and not easy to open in a hurry."

"Let us suppose," said Rolf, "we are going over the wall with a rope. What is next to be considered?"

Chup: "Since the plump wizard here is going with us, I suppose we must consider how to strengthen the strands, with a little magic perhaps." Chup was better suited for this kind of work than any normal man could be; the prospect of desperate action actually cheered him up. Were it not that some in the West still mistrusted the sincerity of his conversion, he would have held a high command. "As he must have done for the backbone of his riding-beast."

Loford did not seem disconcerted. "Would I could strengthen your wits as easily, dull swordsman. About getting away . . . Rolf, is it any clearer now, where the thing must ultimately be taken?"

"Let me think." Trying to find what Ardneh wanted was like trying to find a half-forgotten memory of one's own. Glimmerings came, as if grudgingly. "Farther than we'll be able to ride from here in a single night. More I cannot see."

Loford: "What I am getting at is this. Could not a bird take it? As described, the stone is easily light enough for one to lift."

This time Rolf had to think longer. At last he shook his head. "No. Rather, it will be much better if we do not have to do it that way. Better for it to go by bird than not at all, but . . . it is important also that *I* go, there is some job for me to do, at the same place where the stone is needed." He shook his head again.

Loford scratched his head. "Then we must try to guard you too, and send you on unscratched if possible . . . what is it makes your jaw drop, swordsman? Have you managed a clear thought?''

Chup stopped his fixed staring at the high windows opposite, gave his head a shake, and blinked. ''It may be that today I rode too long staring into the sun. I thought I saw —a woman.''

''Well? And why not?'' Loford asked reasonably.

Chup only shook his head again, and went back to observing the apartment where the High Constable lodged.

Rolf turned to Loford. ''A while ago you said that by tomorrow they may be growing a little careless. But will they not also be on their way?''

''I think not.'' Loford slouched massively on the low windowsill, and with a slight nod indicated the far side of the courtyard. ''A groom has begun paring at the hooves of several of the loadbeasts we followed today.'' That meant no long journey could be contemplated for those animals tomorrow. ''We should have tonight and tomorrow to get ready, and tomorrow night to strike and run.''

They could not decide on a scheme for getting a closer look at the Constable's quarters. After a while Rolf said: ''One of us at least should go to the tavern, hear what the soldiers in the Constable's escort have to say.'' After a moment he added. ''I wish that one of you two would go.''

Chup gave him a quizzical glance. ''Do the painted women make you nervous, young one?''

''No—yes. Because always in the background there's one who owns them. And that people should be owned does bother me, though it seems sometimes not to bother the slaves. I am made nervous in such a way that I want to kill that man.''

Chup emitted a little snort. ''Well, I am not likely to tremble with nervousness in yonder house of joy, nor draw curious glances my way by killing someone. I'll volunteer to go, and brave whatever hardships duty may put in my way.''

When Chup had taken off his sword, and strolled

away, Loford asked: "There is something else we are
to do?"

"I think so. Yes. It will be here in the courtyard—
something or someone that I should watch or wait
for." Not long ago, he would have thought the hunch
was purely his; but he was beginning to grow accustomed to Ardneh's subtlety.

Taking an empty waterbag, Rolf strolled out into
the courtyard, leaving Loford to defend their quarters against sneak thieves or possible late arrivals at
the caravanserai. The scene was generally quiet
now. A servant trotted past on some errand. Animals
made plaintive sounds. A few men, apparently
herdsmen or lower-class traders of some kind,
peered ruminatively from the windows of the lower
rooms. From what Chup had called the house of joy
came a burst of women's laughter, and then the
thumping of a tambourine. Somewhere the
slavemaster would be sitting, his eyes like stone
though his mouth laughed or sipped at wine.

Rolf went to the well, hauled up cold water from
its depths, and drank. He took his time filling the
waterbag. Watching the building in which the Constable was lodged, he saw a pair of white bare feet
descending the uppermost visible portion of the
mostly enclosed stair, bearing above them a
shadowy figure that upon emergence into the
brighter courtyard revealed itself to be that of a
servant girl. She was a tall girl, quite young and
despite her slenderness apparently quite strong;
over her shoulders rode a yoke holding two large
buckets that would be quite weighty when they
were filled. Her hair and dress were both of undis-
tinguished brown, the former bound up out of the
way under a servant's cap. Her face was hard to
judge, its dominant feature at the moment being a
purplish swelling on her cheek that came near to
closing her right eye. At best, Rolf thought, she
would be plain, her nose and mouth being some-

what large though there was prettiness still in the undamaged eye.

Rolf remained standing near the well while he replaced the stopper in his waterbag. The girl approached, set down her yoke, and began working at once to get the buckets filled. The well was equipped with a rope and windlass by which the wayfarer could lower his own container to the water far below. When the girl began to haul up the first heavy pail from the depths of the well, Rolf caught a hint of her exhaustion in the way she leaned against the crank, pausing momentarily after making a beginning against the weight.

Then he put his own burden down, and stepped around the well, saying: "I will lift it."

She stood straight for a moment, looking directly at him—she was a centimeter or two taller than he—without any readable expression in her face. Then she pulled once more on the crank herself.

He put her aside from the windlass, moving himself so firmly into position to turn the crank that she had little choice but to stand aside. Only when he had the filled bucket in his hands did he turn to her again, looking at her carefully for a moment before he set it down and took up the empty one. "You have been ill-used, girl," he said then.

"My mistress insists on being well served," she said steadily, without any obvious feeling of any kind in her voice. Nothing about her speech suggested that she was a servant. There were half-familiar accents in it that Rolf could not quite place at first, until he realized that they reminded him of Duncan's speech, which he had often heard in camp, the tones of the nobility of the Off-Shore Islands in the west.

"I would use you better than she does," he said at once, somewhat surprising himself. He spoke out of policy, of course, offering a drop of sympathy to the maltreated servant in hope of getting some information from her in return; but he meant what he said. And with a faint double shock, two things came to him in rapid sequence; first, that Ardneh had wanted him to go out into the courtyard in order to meet this girl; second, that he had a good idea who her mistress might be, what Lady of the East it was whose servants were more likely than not at any given time to bear the marks of her displeasure, who employed plain-faced maids to make her own great beauty glow the more by contrast.

In the same voice the girl replied: "I doubt that the Lady Charmian would sell me." This only confirmed Rolf's premonition, but still he came near dropping the second water-bucket. Demons of all the East! He must warn Chup before Chup was recognized. But it would hardly do to run away from the girl just yet, when it seemed she might be starting to communicate.

He set the bucket down. "I doubt that I would pay the Lady Charmian in any coin she would willingly accept."

The girl seemed to look more closely and humanly at him then, but only for a moment. Saying nothing, she bent to fasten her buckets to the yoke. When she would have lifted it, however, Rolf stepped in her way again, and with a grunt took up the double load.

"You have been kind," she said, still distantly, "but it will be better for you if you are not seen aiding me. And better for me if I am not seen receiving kindness from a man."

Rolf nodded slowly. "What *will* help you, girl? And what's your name?"

"Catherine, sir. And thank you, but there is no help for me." The calm in her voice was no longer as true as it had been. She came to him and her tall body brushed his as she took the yoke on her own shoulder.

He let it go, but walked beside her as she moved

back toward the stair. "You have not been long in the Lady's service, have you?"

"Not long?" She checked herself. "No — days only, not months or years. What is it to you?" When they reached the bottom of the stairwell they were for the moment alone out of sight of others, and she paused and looked at him somewhat more carefully than before.

Rolf was thinking rapidly. Whether Ardneh was putting his present thoughts into his mind he did not know; certainly he had no feeling of being controlled. "You will not live long in her service. No one does. She will kill you, or cripple you too badly to be of any — no, wait, I am not speaking to torment you. I said that I would use you better. And I will."

She turned her face away, then back to him again. Her whisper was long in coming, but when it came it had a desperate intensity. "There is no way that I can get away from her!"

He kept his own voice low and quick and calm. "And if there were?"

Again Catherine paused. Then: "If she has sent you to entrap me and torment me, I do not care. I must take the chance. I say I will go anywhere, do anything, to get away!"

Now he must think more swiftly still, but now it seemed no help from Ardneh was forthcoming. He could not settle on a detailed plan alone. Feet were moving somewhere above them on the stairs. "Come down again, later. If you can . . . ?"

"There will be more water to be fetched. Slops to be carried out."

"Good. I will meet you, or a friend of mine. He'll call you Catherine, so you know him. Go up now. Have hope."

She gave one abrupt nod and turned her face away, and went on up the stair, despite her burden moving more quickly than she had when coming down.

In the room where he had left Loford waiting, Rolf
saw to his surprise that Chup had returned already,
and was standing against the wall where he could
not be seen from door or window. Rolf had hardly
begun to speak when Chup interrupted him with a
gesture. "Yes, I know my beauteous bride is here,"
he said leaning cautiously toward the window to
glare at the building opposite. "I thought I saw her,
earlier, up there. And then hardly had I gotten into
the funhouse yonder when I saw an Eastern soldier
that I used to know—his mind was on other things,
to our good luck, and I can almost pledge he saw me
not. He was talking to some friend about the Lady
Charmian, enough to make it plain that she is here.
Around my neck like some evil charm she seems to
hang."

"What did you do? Turn in the doorway and come
back?"

"Not quite, for I was fairly in, and to just spin and
run out again might look a little odd. Stood with my
face in a corner, practically, for a while. You might
say that I cut my revelry quite short."

Rolf went to the window for a good look round,
then turned back in. "It seems you were not recognized, or they'd be after us already. Now I've some
better news to tell."

He quickly related to the others his conversation
with Catherine. They resumed their planning, with
at least one of them always watching to see if
Catherine came down again.

The help of Charmian's personal servant should
be a great advantage if only they could hit upon the
most effective way of using her. But whether or not
the jewel was in Charmian's possession or with
some other member of the Constable's party was
still uncertain; the raiders had to make sure of its
location before they could hatch any detailed plan.

When darkness fell it became difficult to see the
stairway from the window of their room, and Rolf
went out into the courtyard and strolled about,

keeping watch. When Catherine came down again, she was carrying pots to be emptied. Rolf walked to intercept her at the refuse pits, which lay at an angle of windowless wall between tavern and stable. It was a dark and noisome place, and for the moment they had it to themselves.

Her face looked fearful, but her gaze did not fall away from his. She said: "If you were joking earlier, tell me now."

"Catherine, I was not. I will take you with me from this place. But there is something else that I must take, and I need your help for that."

"Anything."

"It is probably in your mistress' jewel box, or in the Constable's."

Catherine did not seem in the least surprised. She had had a little time to think things over and form her own idea at what Rolf must want. "The Constable has no strong-box with him, to my knowledge, and I have seen him wear no jewels. I know where the woman's jewel-case lies, but I have never seen it opened . . ."

The lid, massive and strong but elegantly lined within, was standing open at that moment, Charmian having performed the necessary ritual, reciting the three secret words and using the physical key required. She was choosing her jewelry for the evening, while one of her two servant girls, quivering a little as usual, stood by to help with other details.

Considering the hard times that had recently overtaken her, there was a fair amount of wealth and beauty arrayed in the form of bright gems amid the soft compartments of the little chest. In the bottom, looking at odds with everything else, lay a spherical lump of dark stuff the size of a man's two fists. It was mounted in a filigree of silver and gold, no part of which pierced the ebon sphere that it enclosed. As usual, when she looked at it, Charmian frowned; the commander of the cavalry outpost had given it to her, as the best he had to give. No doubt most people would think most of the smaller diamonds more valuable, but Charmian was not so sure; it was quite beautiful in its own different way. But its size! A giantess three meters tall might have worn it as a fine ornament, but what was a woman of ordinary stature to do with such a massive jewel?

She had considered other possibilities, of course. Sensitive to most of the auras of magic, she could feel nothing of power or danger from the thing, no life-potential much above that of any other lump of stone of equal size.

There was a faint sound at her door, the creak of a board under a quiet but heavy tread. The breathing of the maid became suspended, but Charmian did not turn. Let him surprise her thus. Let Abner see how many spaces remained to be filled with wealth inside this one modest treasure-box of hers. While she kept on looking into the box, readying herself to be surprised, she wondered still what the black thing was. When someday she had joined the court of Ominor, when first class wizards were at her service, she would have to have it properly assayed . . .

Abner's great hand came delicately stroking her bare shoulder and she gave a little cry and start, seemingly as spontaneous as the last time he had "surprised" her. She was looking round, her eyes innocently and prettily wide, when his face altered, and his hand on her flesh turned to stone. Her surprise turned real.

He was staring into the open jewel box, and his voice was no longer the voice of an infatuated man, but that of an Eastern Lord. "Where did you get *that*?"

Having seen Catherine back to the foot of the stair, Rolf returned to the room where Chup and Loford waited. There he passed on to them the information that the girl had given. Now in the dust of the floor they could sketch the layout of the rooms in both

Charmian's and the Constable's apartments, and the usual position of the jewel-box in the former. There were other matters to be thought about as well, what soldiers and servants were likely to be where, and how doors were fastened and windows barred. There were a few more questions to be asked of Catherine next time Rolf met with her.

"And one more thing," Chup added. "Do you really mean to bring the girl away with us?"

"We will bring her back to the patrol," said Rolf after a moment. "After that it will be up to Mewick."

Chup nodded slowly. "But if we do not get her clean away, we cannot leave her able to answer questions."

Loford was standing by gloomily, with nothing to say for the moment. Rolf hesitated, but only briefly. "Agreed," he murmured with a nod.

After a moment Chup went on: "Speaking of ladies likely to be thought superfluous, there is the matter of my bride." He fell silent for a little while, staring moodily out the window. Somehow it did not seem to him prohibitively strange to still call Charmian his bride. "I find I do not care if we leave her alive or dead."

The others made no response to that. He felt he could not leave it at that. "Well, I know this is war and not a personal matter . . . I just mean that I will kill her if it seems the best move to make, though I feel no urge to do so."

Still the others remained silent. He himself wondered why he was going on like this about her. Was he making the point that she meant nothing to him one way or the other, or only raising doubts about it?

He had no doubt that she hated him now, that horrible things would happen to him if he ever fell into her power. Well, she was like that. For a time he had hated her, too. Now she was no more important than some poisonous insect, to be avoided or, if the opportunity came, squashed flat.

Rolf and Loford were looking off into space in separate directions, doubtless waiting to make sure that Chup had finished what was for him a lengthy speech.

Loford said at last: "I am glad that your feelings are not involved here." And Rolf: "We will not go out of our way to kill her, then, if she is not at hand when we take the jewel. Of course, if she should get a look at us, it will be better if we do not leave her able to answer questions."

"Of course," said Chup at once. But still he frowned. It was odd. He could picture himself killing Charmian, or almost anyone else. But he could not picture in his mind how she would look when she was dead. Yes, it was odd.

They went back to refining. From all that Catherine had told them, three expertly violent men with the advantage of surprise should be able to get into Charmian's apartment, dispose of the immediate resistance, and get the gem into their hands. When it came to getting away, though, difficulties multiplied.

Chup wished aloud: "If only this girl Catherine could steal the gem for us, bring it out to us."

Loford shook his head. "From what Rolf tells us, there's not a chance of her getting into the treasure box. Charmian's not one to be at all careless with her valuables."

They talked it over, assuming themselves inside the apartment, the jewel in their possession. Now there were poundings on the single door, demands to know what was going on inside.

Chup: "Maybe no one will notice a few screams and a little commotion. That kind of thing's no novelty in my Lady's rooms."

"But suppose they do?"

"Then . . . I wonder if the Constable truly dotes on her? I wonder if she could serve us as a hostage?"

That idea and others were debated. The discus-

sion went on far into the night, when it was set aside
for rest. The three men took turns at watching
throughout the remainder of the night.

Shortly before dawn, Loford strolled outside as if
to stretch some stiffness from his limbs. There, as
pre-arranged with Mewick, he spelled out the essentials of the plan they had decided on, using gestures natural to a man who had waked up with some
aching joints. They meant to be coming out from the
rooftop tomorrow night, with the gem in their possession. He hoped that his gestures were being
watched by one of the great birds, circling on
hushed wings well above the walls. If they were
lucky, a bird or two had been able to join Mewick's
patrol tonight.

The remainder of the night passed uneventfully,
and so did the greater portion of the following day.
Late in the afternoon Catherine made what would
be, if things went well, her final trip down to the
well. This time Rolf did not meet her, but watched
from the concealment of his room as she gave the
unobtrusive signal meaning that nothing had arisen
to require a change in plans or a final consultation.
As expected, the Constable's party showed no signs
of leaving. They had been on the road for many days,
and men and beasts alike were doubtless ready for a
day of rest.

Night fell, and in their little ground-floor room
three merchants became Western warriors once
more, removing extra weapons and equipment from
their packs to be distributed about their persons,
then covered with long travelers' cloaks. Then there
was nothing to do but hold final vigil at the window.

Time dragged. Chup was just beginning to ask:
"Are you sure that she will come—" when there she
came, Catherine emerging from the dark mouth of
the stair opposite, making her way across the ill-lit
courtyard. She too had put on a long cloak, but her
feet were still bare. Rolf hoped she was carrying at

least a pair of sandals for the trip; there was no way to be sure when they would meet Mewick and the others and be able to ride.

The plan called for her to come to them openly, as if she had been sent to the three merchants with a message.

"Gentlemen, you are asked to come," she said in a low voice when she had reached their open door.

"Asked?" Rolf echoed. He was not sure for the moment whether Catherine was only playing her role, or whether Abner or Charmian actually wanted to see the "merchants" about something.

"It is I who ask you," she said with feeling, looking from one of them to the other. The hood of her cloak was thrown back, and her brown hair was looser than it had been. Her eye looked a little puffier, if anything, than yesterday.

"We are ready for some bargaining," said Rolf, and stepped forward to the doorway and took her gently by the elbow, both to reassure her and to keep her from turning thoughtlessly and starting back at once—the three merchants must take a little time to ask a question or two, gather their sample wares, see to their own appearance, before calling on such an eminent lady. Catherine's arm had a lifeless submissiveness in Rolf's grip; it was a feeling that he had met before, on touching slaves, slaves who had had reason to take him for an Eastern master. It came to Rolf that in a sense this girl had now become his slave, his property, and there was a twinge of forbidden pleasure in the thought.

The proper moments for delay soon passed, and the four of them set out across the courtyard, the three men unhurriedly walking ahead.

"I could learn nothing more that will be helpful," the girl whispered to Rolf, from her position close behind him.

"All right." He tried to sound calm and reassuring. "Do what I say, without hesitating. We will bring you out."

A moment more and they were ascending the
stairs of the building in which Charmian and the
Constable were lodged. As they passed the open
doorway of a second-floor apartment, through
which several junior officers of the East could be
seen gaming around a table, Loford said, as though
continuing a conversation: " . . . we can procure
what your Lady wants, if we have it not in the goods
we carry with us. We stand ready at any hour of the
day or night to serve so illustrious . . ." He let his
voice fade to a meaningless mumble as they passed
the door and started up the next-to-final flight of
stairs. The uppermost flight, and the doors and
landing at its top, were still invisible. As they turned
the corner and started up the final flight the expected sentry at the top came into view, looking
down coldly at them.

"Right up to the top, your honors, please," said
Catherine clearly from just behind Rolf, and could
not keep the strain out of her voice. Behind the
sentry were the two doors she had described to Rolf;
the right one would lead to the Constable's quarters, the left to the Lady Charmian's. From behind
the right door male voices could be heard, in low
and serious talk, too muffled for words to be distin-
guishable.

The sentry was Rolf's to cope with, for Chup's
greater effectiveness with the sword might be
needed to meet the unexpected at one door or the
other, and Loford might be needed just as suddenly
for magical action and was too clumsy in any case to
be trusted with a knifing.

On the topmost landing the men stood awkwardly, for it was not large, and the cold-eyed guard
refused to give much ground. He was not truly suspicious yet. Catherine slid among the men to Charmian's door, to tap and call softly. It seemed Charmian did not like even her maids to take her by
surprise. Rolf stood rigidly waiting until he heard
the bar lifted inside the door, then saw the door

open a crack to frame the eye of another servant girl inside; he turned then, with unhurried smoothness that was practised but still not easy, not for him, brought a long dagger from under his cloak without any unnecessary flourishes, and pushed it up firmly beneath the sentry's breastbone.

The sound life made in going out was not loud, and was covered by the whimpering little cry of the surprised servant-girl as Chup pushed in the door she had unlocked, and pushed his way inside, Loford right on his heels. Rolf with his unarmed hand caught his falling victim around the waist, and half-carried, half-dragged the dying man along into the apartment. Catherine, still waiting at the door, pulled it shut and barred it once everyone was inside.

Chup and Loford were not pausing, but strode on ahead of Rolf across the little dingy room, toward the one door on its farther side, their heavy soft treads shaking the floor slightly, setting muted jinglings sounding amid the feminine trappings hanging in an open portable wardrobe. The maidservant who had opened the door was still cowering on the floor where Chup had shoved her, paralyzed with shock and fright. Rolf let his murdered sentry down, showed the girl the bloody knife, whispered in her ear: "One squeak and we will cut your throat," and pushed her into the big wardrobe amid the hanging garments, where she fell to the floor in what was almost silence. He flashed a look of reassurance to Catherine, still leaning on the barred door, and turned after Chup and Loford who were entering the other room.

Some sound, or instinct, must have warned the Lady Charmian. When her husband and the men behind him came through the one door of her little bedchamber, she was standing as if waiting for them. She wore a long, soft lounging garment of some pink satiny stuff; her feet were bare on a soft, thick black rug that must have come to this place with her. The incredible golden cascade of her hair hung well below her waist. Rolf saw her eyes of melting blue, familiar as if he had last seen them only an hour before, go wide as she recognized Chup.

"Silence gives life," Chup told her briefly, and went past her to the strongbox, which was just where Catherine had said that it would be, standing on a low, crude chest just below the high window with its heavy bars. Chup flicked the side of the box with his swordpoint, once, hesitantly, felt the muted shock of guardian powers, and drew quickly back. Loford shouldered past him to bend over the box, mumbling. Chup moved to where he could watch Charmian and at the same time look back into the outer room of the apartment, where Catherine still waited with her back against the door. Rolf, standing in the doorway between the rooms, could see and feel the mutual hatred pass between her and Charmian.

And now Charmian's eyes, with a different look, reached for Rolf's eyes, brushed them once, then fell away, very quickly and shyly. No, her eyes said, it was useless to try to beguile him. She had been too cruel to him long ago; and that was sad beyond bearing, because now, looking back, Charmian could see that he was the one man with whom she might have been happy.

She said it all with that one glance, no matter that it was all impossible nonsense. The falsity of it was irrelevant while she was saying it.

Loford had turned and was extending a massive hand toward the Lady Charmian. "The key," he said, in almost courtly tones. The strongbox now looked a little larger, the shape of it was somewhat altered, since the wizard had bent over it.

"You are but bandits, then," Charmian said, while her hand made slow searching motions among the pockets of her robe, as if to find a key. "I warned my Lord the Constable to give more thought to such.

Now perforce he will admit that I was right." Rolf understood that she was bargaining for her life, telling them as well as she could in the hearing of the servant in the wardrobe, that they would not be named by her as Western soldiers if they would spare her life.

She might be able to make almost anything believable. "I would that you were more than bandits," she went on, speaking now to Chup, with eyes again as well as words. "I dreamt once that a man had come to carry me away, so that from that day on I would never have to serve another man but him. And in that dream —"

"The key," Chup grated in an ugly voice. "Or I will spoil your lying face." Charmian knew him. She seemed to collapse before the threat, shrinking back against the wall.

"The key is in the bedside table," she said simply.

Chup kept his eyes on her until Loford had gone to the chest with the key and come back holding up the dark round thing in its silver filigree. Rolf had never seen anything just like it before, but felt Ardneh's certainty that it was the right thing. Rolf nodded, then added: "Don't forget the rest."

They had discussed this point beforehand, too. If they were to be taken for bandits they must not leave a single jewel that they could carry away. Loford went to scoop up other wealth from the box, and stuff his pockets with it. The black jewel, meanwhile, he had tossed to Rolf, who put it into a small empty pouch that waited ready at his belt.

There came a startling, though quiet, trying of the outer door, followed after a moment by a rattling and wrenching that made it thud against its hinges. An indistinct male voice called out, in what might have been anger or alarm. The absence of the sentry from the stair would certainly awaken Eastern vigilance.

Chup's eyes were still riveted on Charmian's. In a low voice he demanded: "Is that the Constable?"

She gave a little shiver, an involuntary movement that Rolf thought he had seen her make once before, when men were about to kill each other for her amusement. It seemed a joyous movement. She said: "It is his way; it sounds like him."

Rolf stepped quietly back to Catherine and took her by the arm. "Let me get in place behind the door," he whispered. "Then open it and let him—" He broke off there, for outside at least one more heavy voice had joined the Constable's, and the tramp of yet other feet was somewhere on the stair.

Pulling Catherine by the arm, he hurried to the inner room again. There was only the one door, and the windows were narrow and heavily barred. It was well they had made alternate plans. Loford had his sword out and was digging an escape hole in the flimsy ceiling; in a moment Rolf was working at his side. Dried mud fell in his face, and lengths of reed and sapling began to dangle brokenly.

The noise at the door turned into a determined assault. Chup said something that Rolf could not hear to Charmian. Charmian turned to the door and cried out loudly: "Stop! These men will kill me if you force your way in. Stop, they wish to bargain with you!"

The banging and chopping ceased. "Bargain?" roared a man's deep voice. "With what? Who are they, what do they want?"

"They are bandits," Charmian cried weakly. Glancing toward her, Rolf saw that she had retreated from Chup's sword until her head was pressed against the wall, but the sword had advanced until it now poised rock-steady a centimeter from her face. Loss of beauty would be worse than loss of life to her.

There was a pause outside, as if of disbelief. "Well, wondrous stupid ones, so it would seem." More feet now on the stair, a platoon gathering hurriedly; and overhead now, soft footsteps on the roof; it had not taken the Constable long to order his forces. Now he

bellowed, with vast authority: "Ho, in there! The
trap is shut on you; unbar this door!" Chup forced
his erstwhile bride into the big wardrobe where one
of her servant-girls was still cowering in silence.
What he said to Charmian at parting Rolf could not
hear, but she went in with quiet alacrity.

Loford had ceased prying at the ceiling, and
sheathed his sword, but stood still looking upward
at the damage while he made the gestures of his
magic art. Now he signed to Rolf to cease work also;
Rolf did so. But by Loford's art, the noises they had
made when working went right on without a pause,
the subdued splintering of light wood, the trickling
falls of powdery fragments to the floor were heard,
though the hole they had begun in the roof now got
no bigger. Now Rolf attacked the floor with his dagger. He labored to pry up a board; Catherine dropped to her knees beside him and wrenched with
strong sure hands as soon as he had raised one end
enough for her to get a purchase on it. By the art of
Loford, who worked on silently above them, the
shriek of yielding nails was made to come from
overhead.

The Constable's voice renewed its demands for
entry.

"Not so fast!" Chup roared back. "What'll you give
us for your woman's life?" And he thumped with the
flat of his sword on the wardrobe, from which the
voice of Charmian hastily called out, serving to
demonstrate that she was still alive.

Rolf and Catherine by this time had one floor-
board completely up. A quick look down through
the gap assured him that the room below was deserted. The soldiers lodged in it would have been
called to duty when the alarm broke out.

The Constable's overbearing voice called out
some threat, and the battering at the door resumed,
more violently than before. The renewed noise from
the door, with that induced by magic overhead, effectively covered the ripping up of another board.

The whole was big enough now for Rolf, and he was through it in a moment, with Catherine right behind him. Loford had to tear up yet another plank before the gap was wide enough to accommodate his bulk; luckily the ceilings were low and he had not far to fall. Chup was right behind.

Catherine picked up a bow, and looped over her shoulder a quiver of arrows that had been left in a corner of the room. With her cloak she might manage to conceal the weapons, and she pulled up its hood now to hide her face. Rolf was at the door, peering out through a crack until one set of hurried footsteps had passed their landing going up, and another down; and then he led the way out onto the stair, flattening himself against a wall. The Constable's men were gathered on the stair and landing above, still assaulting the heavy door of the top-floor apartment.

Rolf, Catherine, Loford, Chup. In single file on the stair, the four of them glided swiftly down. At the bottom of the stair, weapons under cloaks, they passed out swiftly through the doorway into the courtyard where torches flared, disturbed animals stamped and moved and grunted, and travelers, slaves, grooms, tavern girls, all milled around, gaping upward with mixed alarm and interest.

The four moved in a regular walking pace across the courtyard to the stair on the other side; over there was the only way out. They were about half-way across, moving deliberately amid people and restless animals, when behind them Charmian's screams for help were suddenly added to the noise. She must have at last dared to peer out of the wardrobe, to find herself practically alone amid unnerving sounds. When the screams came Rolf took Catherine's arm in a hard grip, but he need not have bothered, for her step remained steady. Without interference from anyone in the ragged little crowd of gapers, the four reached the desired doorway and began to mount the stair. This building was less solidly built than the one they had just come from, though of the same general plan.

Doors stood open to their right and left as they ascended, one floor, two, but for the moment no one was in sight. The rooms had evidently been emptied of soldiers and onlookers alike by the alarms.

Now Chup took the lead, and pulled back the hood of his cloak. As they rounded the last landing going up, the expected sentry appeared at the top of the stair, the door to the room behind him standing open.

Chup in his best Eastern-officer voice demanded: "Here, fellow, are any men loitering in those rooms?" and kept on climbing as he spoke.

"No, sir! No malingerers here."

"Then who is that?" Chup barked. He pointed behind the sentry into a dark corner of an empty room as he came up to the man, bringing a sure blade from beneath his cloak as the man's head turned.

Now, the four could go unhurriedly up a ladder from the topmost stair-landing to a trapdoor that opened on the roof. Rolf, once more in the lead, flattened himself down as he crawled out into the open night. On the roof across the court the Eastern men waiting in fruitless ambush were being less cautious, and he could see them easily in silhouette. All was quiet in that direction now, a state of affairs that could not last much longer; the Constable would be finding his trap empty, and would be howling on their trail when he saw the great hole they had made in the floor.

Chup had the soft thin coil of rope unwound from his midsection, and now lay on his back with his feet against the low parapet, making himself a human anchor to hold the rope while the others slid down. Rolf went first. The rope was long enough to reach the ground with a little to spare. As soon as sand was under his feet, he tugged once on the rope and waited with drawn sword. Catherine came next, dropping her bow when halfway down but picking it up before she scrambled to Rolf's side; and then Loford, grunting and mumbling as the rope burned his sliding fingers. Then came the rope itself, a whispering coil; then Chup, dropping unaided from rooftop to sand.

IV

Distance

————◆—◆◆—◆————

In single file the four of them marched in silence,
save for the soft crunch underfoot of sand, and the
faint whisper of the wind. Now Loford followed Rolf,
and then the girl, with Chup alert to hear pursuers
in the rear. They left the caravanserai kilometers
behind, while the stars spun slowly around the one
that marked the Pole. Rolf strode on into the unknown with confidence, though he had only a hazy
idea of what kind of country lay in that direction,
and no idea at all of the goal that Ardneh wanted
him finally to reach. No one spoke, except that once
or twice a faint whisper-mutter with the rhythm of
magic in it came forward to Rolf's ears, and soon
thereafter arose what might have been perfectly
natural pushes of wind against their faces, wind
howling back down along their trail with strength
enough to pull sand over their footprints.

Rolf now and again looked up, trying to catch
sight of wide bird-wings against the stars. But there
were none.

"We had best get clear of this open sand before
morning," Chup growled once, low-voiced, from the
rear. Rolf only grunted in reply. The need was obvious. Rolf stepped up his pace a little more. Now he
could hear Catherine's breathing. But the girl kept
up without faltering.

The hours of the night turned on. There was no
pause for rest. No hint of dawn had yet appeared in
the clear sky when Rolf noticed that the character of
the country was changing. The gentle dunes grew

steeper, and among them there jutted up hillocks and humps of worn, eroded clay. Grass and bushes, appeared in a thin scattering, then became noticeably thicker. As the eastern sky began to brighten subtly, the clay hills came to dominate the land. These turned into a plateau across which the travelers walked, scrambling frequently through small ravines that lay across their path, or following those that ran for a time along it. Some of these narrow ravines were steep enough to have small overhangs along their sides, and these, when the morning sky began to brighten up in earnest, afforded some possibility of hiding for the day.

Rolf chose a place, which was then improved by digging back a little into the clay bank, the excavated material being carefully scattered where it would not show. Now, lying on the narrow ledge that they had made, it was possible to see back for nearly a kilometer in the way that they had come, and for some forty or fifty meters along the ravine in the other direction. And from this direction, now, at last, came Mewick and the other members of the patrol; or most of them, rather. There were five riders, not six, approaching.

The four who had just lain down in weariness sprang up again. Mewick reined in below their ledge, saying: "The birds have just now gone to shelter for the day. We would have caught up with you sooner, but—" He made a gesture of weariness, dismissing causes pointless to enumerate now. He and his mount, and the men and animals behind him, looked tired, and some had new bandages to show. "There is cavalry on your trail, not two kilometers back. They dared to follow you out by night, and we were not enough for a real ambush. We only delayed them a little and I lost Latham."

It registered now with Rolf whose face was missing, whose animal was being led in the rear with the other spares. The shock of a friend's loss came and was set aside in the pile of losses that must someday be dealt with somehow. Now Rolf only asked: "How many of them?" As he spoke he was packing his meager gear into a roll, getting ready to bundle it onto the back of the best spare riding-beast.

"Fifty. Thereabouts," said Mewick wearily. "Through divination or otherwise they must have some inkling of the importance of what you took; else I think they would not have come onto your trail at night, no. The Constable is leading them in person. Has Ardneh any offering of guidance now?"

"Only that I must go on, with what I carry." Rolf finished tying his bundle onto the beast and swung himself up into its saddle. His eye fell on Catherine, and saw in her a desperation made calm only by her great weariness. The mention of Ardneh had probably meant nothing to her, he realized. Most probably she feared only one thing more than being with this bandit gang—there was still no reason for her to think them anything but bandits—and that one thing was being left behind by them, to be retaken by the East. "Mount up, girl," he ordered, pointing to another ready animal. "Come with me." Only after he had spoken did he realize that there was a deeper purpose than compassion, or any selfish want, behind his words.

Mewick raised his eyebrows, then nodded, handing Rolf provisions and a water bag. "So it must be. We here will do what must be done. Which way does Ardneh bid you go? We will try to turn the ones who follow aside."

"I am still heading just a little west of north. I *think* it will be many days yet before I reach the goal—whatever it may be."

Mewick and others raised their hands, murmuring good wishes. Arrangements for future contact would be left to nighttime and the birds—or to Ardneh, if he should take a hand overtly. Rolf dug heels into his mount and set off along the ravine to the north; a glance back showed Catherine riding

competently and close behind him. If, as her accent
suggested, she were really of some noble family in
the Offshore Islands, it was natural that she should
know how to ride.

The cleft of the ravine grew shallow, and bent off
in the wrong direction. Rolf heeled his riding-beast
to a faster pace as he urged it out onto the flat
surface of a plateau. Steadily they put distance between themselves and the place behind them where
Mewick was trying to arrange an ambush of an
enemy force that outnumbered his by something
more than five to one. Rolf knew that Mewick and his
six men would not stand and be wiped out, not if
they could help it. They would strike and retreat
and strike again, if they were able. If they could get
through the day, the night would offer better hope.
But it was early morning now . . .

Rolf and his companion had come about a kilometer across the open plateau, and were almost in
reach of another favorably oriented ravine, offering
some chance of shelter from the sky, when there
came drifting from a height the raucous cry that
meant they had been spotted by a reptile.

No use to gallop now; Rolf held to a steady pace.
The reptile was overtaking them on effortless wings,
staying high out of bowshot; directly over their
heads, it marked their position for the pursuers on
the ground.

When Rolf and Catherine topped a slight rise,
they could look back and see the mounted Eastern
force, coming now onto the broken plateau, nearing
the place where Mewick and the others must be in
wait. It seemed the ambush could be no surprise, for
there were more reptiles, concentrating over something Rolf could not see—over seven Western soldiers, no doubt. He felt an urge, not courageous but
simply irrational, to turn back and be with them. But
that was not to be.

Catherine drew abreast of him as they rode on.
She asked: "Your whole band is scattering in dif-

ferent directions?'' When he did not answer, she
asked him: ''What did he call you back there?
Ardneh?''

''My name is Rolf.''

''Rolf, then. There is something I would ask of
you.''

''Wait.'' He urged his mount over a difficult
stretch of terrain, then stopped for a brief halt, to
rest the animals for the space of a few breaths and to
see by what route the pursuing cavalry was following. ''Now. What was it?''

Catherine said: ''If we are going to be taken by
them, kill me first.''

It was only surprising for a moment. ''If that time
ever comes, I will have other matters to think about.
But cheer up, it has not come yet.''

The enemy riders had turned suddenly away from
what seemed their logical course, and were slowing
down. No reason was visible at this distance; but
the concentration of reptiles, somewhat nearer,
seemed greatly agitated. The one who had been flying directly over Rolf and Catherine, evidently assuming that they could be found again without any
trouble on this bright morning, suddenly darted
back to join the others.

''Now!'' Seizing the chance for whatever it might
prove to be worth, Rolf turned his beast off running
at a tangent to the course they had been following.
He had begun to alter his true course, a little west of
north, as soon as he thought the leatherwings had
spotted them, and now he took it up again. And now,
far ahead, he could already see how the country
shaded out of barren badlands and into a higher
and grassier plateau.

The moments of freedom from reptile observation
fled by, and Rolf could make no profit from them.
There was no reasonable place of concealment in
sight, nowhere they could vanish, to be gone when
the reptile came back to find them, as it must. As he

rode, Rolf anxiously tried to reach Ardneh's thought, to find guidance. Nothing helpful came, nothing except the impression of a titanic weariness: a vague image of a faceless, beleaguered giant, hard pressed by a thousand enemies. What Rolf was doing was important, and worthy of Ardneh's help, but no more so than ten or a score of other struggles in which Ardneh was simultaneously involved. At this moment there could be no help for Rolf, except the continuing sense of the direction he was to travel.

The summer day stretched long ahead of them, before the night would bring a reasonable chance of shelter and of rest. Again there sounded the shouts of men at war, louder than might have been expected when fifty were facing only seven. Looking back, Rolf saw a gray maelstrom of wind and dust settling upon, or very near, the area where the fighting must have been. Loford must have managed to raise a desert-elemental. The Eastern troops would be powerless to advance as long as it blasted and blinded them with sand, but the Constable would be sure to have able magical assistance with him and the elemental might be soon dispersed. Meanwhile, the reptiles were being driven from the fighting by the terrific winds; now instead they came on after Rolf and the girl.

Given a great-enough advantage in numbers, the leatherwings were willing to attack armed humans and there were a score or more of them now in sight. Rolf asked: "Can you use that stick of wood you carry?"

Catherine unslung the bow from her back and groped for an arrow, meanwhile guiding her mount with her knees. "Once I could shoot with some skill. It has been a long time since I had the chance."

Rolf grunted. He was an indifferent archer, but almost certainly he would do better than she with sword.

The reptiles circled them at low altitude, a ragged-looking swirl of gray-green wings and yellow teeth; then, from all points of the compass at once, they closed. Catherine's first arrow missed, but she had time for a second, and one of the creatures tumbled heavily into the sand, a clean kill. Then the cawing cloud engulfed the riders. Rolf swung his blade with brutal energy. The riding-beasts plunged and screamed when they felt teeth and talons. Again and again Rolf's sword met resistance, parting leathery hide, stringy flesh, and light bones. Then suddenly the flock was gone, those who could still fly whirling at a safe distance to screech their rage, leaving half a dozen dead and wounded to litter the thirsty sand. Catherine had sheltered under her great cloak when the enemy came within clawing range, and she was unscratched though the cloak had been rent in several places. Nor was Rolf injured, but the animals, shivering and muttering, were each bleeding from several wounds.

Still, the riding-beasts trudged stolidly on, and this was not the time and place to stop and tend them if it could be avoided. Rolf was momentarily expecting the enemy cavalry to come into sight, the elemental had perhaps been dispersed, though a pall of dust still hanging over the area made it difficult to see what was going on back there. But no riders appeared. Once again, fainter than before, Rolf heard the sounds of fighting. Time was being bought for his escape, at what cost he did not care to think.

The reptiles continued in their circle. Catherine rode silently at his side, watching them with her chin up, an arrow nocked and ready in her bow.

The morning progressed, the reptiles gradually withdrawing farther and at last breaking their circle and landing, one of their number remaining airborne to observe Rolf and Catherine from a distance. Rolf called a rest stop, and devoted it mainly to caring for the animals, whose wounds were bloodier than he had thought. Insects were buzzing around them already. With Catherine helping efficiently, he did what he could to clean the wounds, and bandaged those in places where a bandage could be made secure. Then the two humans walked on for a while, leading the animals, before remounting.

Considering the damage the reptiles had suffered in their first attack, Rolf was not surprised that they forebore to launch another. When about midday they returned in a menacing cloud, Catherine loosed another arrow at them. They clamored insults but flew no closer.

Slowly but steadily the kilometers flowed by beneath the plodding beasts. Twice during the afternoon Rolf halted to rest and tend the animals as well as possible, and for long stretches he and Catherine walked. Far behind, there was still dust on the horizon. He groped for Ardneh's presence once more, and this time received a feeling of reassurance; help was to be granted, or was being granted now. What kind of help was not explained, but Rolf felt somewhat easier. He was further cheered when at last the reptiles screamed their final insults and began their forced retreat, to the safe roosts they must seek out before the coming of the night.

Rolf shortly called a halt. The mounts were swaying and stumbling with fatigue, and the place they had come to offered grazing as promising as any they were likely to find. It was a nearly dried-out watercourse, marked along its edges by abundant grass, a few bushes, and even scattered trees.

The animals' wounds included several ugly punctures that seemed likely to become infected. When they had done what they could for the beasts, and eaten a little themselves, it had grown dark. "Rest," Rolf grunted. Catherine, looking too tired to answer, collapsed into a silent heap.

He was too tired himself to try to stay awake when the likelihood of an enemy coming seemed vanishingly small. He arranged his weapons handily and began to doze off in the warm night, his back against the curved bank of the dry channel. Vaguely he wondered about Catherine, how she had come to be a slave, what she would want . . . he was too sleepy to think long.

Waking abruptly to the racketing of insects, he quickly surveyed the night-world about him before he moved. The starry powder of the Milky Way made a vast diagonal blaze across the sky. It took a second or two before he saw what had somehow awakened him. Perched high on the opposite bank of the ravine, a great bird rested motionless, its feathered bulk cutting a dark pattern from the light of stars. When Rolf turned his head toward the bird he saw the huge wings open and reach out, balancing, far wider than a man's spread arms.

Its voice was musical, and so soft he had to listen carefully to make sure of all the words. "Rooolf of the Brooken Lands, rest no moore this night. Those who pursue you are not far away, and they will come on with the first of the morning light."

Rolf glanced up at the stars to gauge the time. He had only slept for three or four hours, but felt considerably refreshed. The riding-beasts, used to birds, were dozing on their feet where he had picketed them a little distance off. He got to his feet and began to gather his few belongings. He asked the bird: "What of my friends who fought to buy me time?"

"The one whoo spoke to me was a tall, fat wizard," the bird replied. "He said to tell yoooou that Metzgar had fallen, but that the others fared well enough."

"Ah." Tall Metzgar, of the long beard, and long stories . . .

"Also I must tell youuu that more friends, and enemies, are beginning to move into this country from the south. But all of them are kilometers and kilometers away as yet. Also, Duncan wants to know what you are doooing now."

"Tell Duncan I am going on," said Rolf. He shot a quick look at Catherine, but she gave no sign of having moved since she lay down. He introspected for a moment, and found something new. "And tell Duncan, and the fat wizard, that now I must angle more toward the West. I am going to travel an hour or so and try to hide again before dawn. If the pursuers can be led straight on north, or east, it will be a considerable help."

The bird hooted once, assentingly, then rose with a silent effort and disappeared among the stars, just as Catherine stirred. A moment later she sat up, looking groggy and bewildered.

"Get up," he ordered. "We have more distance to cover before the dawn." She sighed and got to her feet slowly but without complaint. Only now did he notice that she had evidently not managed to find a pair of sandals. Well, if the animals held out, it would make little difference.

There was not much water left in the bag, but the country was no longer desert-dry and Rolf was not much concerned on that account. The animals seemed strong enough, but restless, as if their wounds were paining them. Catherine dozed in the saddle from time to time; Rolf would see her head start to sink forward, then jerk erect as she caught herself into wakefullness. It was not a good time for talking; the ears had to be kept free for more important matters.

Before the sky had begun to pale in the east, they came to another mud-bottomed creek bed. This was wider than the last one and filled with tall, reedy flowers. These were full-leaved enough in places to form fairly secure screens against aerial observation. Rolf made a screen for the animals against the high bank of the dry creek, under which they were willing enough to lie when he had given them some water. He and Catherine found dry spots close together at a little distance from the animals, and after bending a few flower-stalks overhead for better concealment lay down and promptly slept.

When Rolf awoke again the sun was full and
bright, hurling splinters of its light between leaves
into his face. Insects murmured undisturbed in the
full drowse of summer day. The girl, curled up in her
brown servant's dress, face hidden resting on her
rolled-up cloak, still slept. Her back was to Rolf, her
breathing regular, her legs pulled up inside her
dress. He noticed that the bottoms of her bare feet
were calloused hard.

He arose silently and went on a brief scouting
expedition, fifty meters or so up and down the
mud-bottomed gully, not getting far from the tall
flowers. He studied the sky with great care but saw
no reptiles. He found a place where it seemed a little
digging might reach water. And he stood looking
long to the northwest. There were some trees in that
direction, and a great deal of long grass, but the
cover seemed inadequate for an attempt at traveling
by day. They had finally managed to lose the enemy
and there was no sense in being spotted again at
once. He tried to weigh in his mind the odds that the
Constable would bring his men this way, find the
creek-bed, follow it, and flush them out, before
darkness fell again.

He could hope that Ardneh would warn him again
in time, but he could not be sure. It seemed to him
that he had scores of kilometers yet to travel.

He went quietly back to Catherine, who had
stirred in her sleep, stretched out her legs, and
turned her face up. Now she looked very young. Her
face was not pretty, he thought, even apart from the
still-swollen and discolored cheekbone and a few
odd scratches and smears acquired in the last day
and night. Her nose was just off-shape enough to
deny her prettiness in any case. And her stretched-
out body now looked a little awkward.

But she was most certainly a girl. He had not had
the leisure until now to consciously consider her as
such.

An insect whirred close above her face. Waking suddenly, she sat up with a start, regarded him with bewilderment for a moment, and then sank back, remembering.

"I have got away from her," she said then, softly, looking all around as if awakening from some evil dream, and making sure of reality. Then she looked at Rolf and added: "Your friends have not caught up with us. Are we to meet them somewhere?"

"Nor my enemies, either." He regarded her silently for a few moments. "Your black eye looks better than it did."

Her gaze dropped as if in sudden shyness. "What will we do now?"

"Eat some food. Dig a hole in this mud, we'll probably be able to get some drinkable water. It may take a while, but we'll be here all day with little else to do. Don't want to travel with the reptiles watching, not once we've lost them."

She got up stiffly, brushing back from her eyes long hair that had come unbound. "Shall I start digging right away?"

"See about getting a little food ready. I'll dig. The animals are going to need more water soon."

Rolf took a long knife and dug for a while in the likeliest-looking place he could fnd, a sandy area against a bank. At first only soupy muck appeared, but after some diligence in scooping out the hole and patience in letting it refill, a supply of usable water was available. After he led the animals to drink, he and Catherine sat eating dried food and finishing the contents of the waterbag.

She was not very talkative, he thought. In fact it seemed to him that the silence was definitely growing awkward, before she suddenly announced: "I am sure that my family will pay some ransom for me if you were to find a way of returning me to the Offshore Islands. We are not poor, and our city was never overrun by the East."

Rolf munched for a while in thoughtful silence.

The less he told her now, the better, he decided. She might become separated from him in some way, and fall again into Eastern hands. He said: "It doesn't seem likely that I'll be able to take you home. Not very soon."

Eagerly she edged a little closer to him, again putting back her long brown hair. "You wouldn't have to take me all the way. If you could show me how I can reach one of the armies of the West, I would—I would pledge that my family would reward you." When he was silent her eagerness faded. "I know, it would mean having to wait for your money. And why should you believe me at all?"

"I have heard your accent before. I believe you, about your family. But I have other business that must be taken care of, that cannot wait."

She said no more for a while. But after they had led the animals back to deeper shelter, she said: "I do not know if you are waiting here for your friends, or what. I suppose you don't want to tell me."

Rolf threw himself down in the spot where he had slept, and after a moment Catherine sat nearby, next to her rolled-up cloak. She went on: "Maybe you have to divide your loot with them. I don't know how such things are managed among bandits. But if you are not planning to meet them, or if you have given them up for lost, then you might come with me, and join the West. I am sure that they need sturdy men."

"Hm. Or even if I wanted to run out on my friends, not split the loot with them at all, I could do that." He paused, wickedly enjoying her confusion. "But there are good reasons why I cannot do that. Not right now."

She was downcast, but persistent. "I understand, you have that great jewel to profit from. Why should you get mixed up in battles? Maybe you even were once a Western soldier, and deserted. I know some men become bandits that way. I do not know or care, I only know that you have helped me more than you can know, and I want to thank you for it. Since you have done it, for whatever reason, you might as well have the reward. My father is a burgomaster of Birgun, which as you may know is one of the chief cities of the Offshore Islands, a city never touched by the East and still powerful. Prince Duncan's home is not far from there, and I am sure that you have heard of him."

"A friend of yours, no doubt."

"I have seen him. Not much more than that."

"If your city was untouched, how did you come to be a slave?"

She looked off into the distance. "A long story, like many others you must know. I was traveling away from home, and caught up in an Eastern raid . . . I am sure my kinsmen must be searching for me, and their gratitude will be great toward anyone who brings me back." Her eyes came back to Rolf. "And no one in the Islands would think you a thief for having taken some Eastern jewels at the same time."

Both were silent for a little while. Then Catherine went on, as if more to herself than to Rolf: "There is also the man to whom I was pledged in marriage, but it has been so long . . . more than a year since I was lost. He may well be married to another by now, or dead, for he was a soldier." She seemed calm enough about it, as if all that former life were decades behind her instead of only months; and Rolf understood her; his life too had been broken off in the same way.

Evidently encouraged because he was at least tolerating her talk, she asked: "Do you know anything of how the war is going?"

He thought a little, and made an answer that any alert bandit should be able to give. "Duncan keeps an army in the field, keeps the fight going. Ominor can't seem to drive him off the mainland, or plant him in it either."

A sparkle shown in Catherine's good eye. "I tell

you, the West is going to win. If they have not been beaten by this time, it never can be done."

"The same thing might be said about the East," Rolf said drowsily, and closed his eyes. "I'll think on what you've said. No more of it for now. Try and get some more sleep. Later in the day the Constable may be coming near, and we'll need to be alert."

They spent the remaining daylight hours in their hideaway, resting, watching, trying to help the animals. The beasts were in pain from their infected wounds, and one of them was limping noticeably. Rolf glimpsed a reptile in the distant sky, but he could not tell what business it was about. In the last hour before sunset he grew restless and impatient, listening intently at every far-off sound. As soon as it was dark, having eaten again, they set off into the northwest, leading the animals until the day's stiffness should be worked out of their muscles.

At the first rest stop the girl said to him: "Let me ask you bluntly. Do you mean to keep me with you? What will you do with me?"

"Have I not used you better than your previous master did? Of course. What are you worried about? The less you know of my business, the better off you are, I think."

"I see that." She spoke softly and reasonably. "It is only that I have hopes of traveling west, of getting home. I did think of running away from you, but I do not fear you anymore. And I know nothing of the land here, or where the armies are."

"Let me think about it, I say again. Don't worry. You are not getting any farther from your goal."

For the remainder of the night Catherine said no more about her hopes and fears, and had very little to say on any subject. Rolf set a steady pace that covered a good many kilometers, though now both animals were limping and the humans walked more than they rode. Toward dawn they came upon a running stream with tree-lined banks. After drinking their fill, they were searching for some good cover against the coming hours of daylight, when out of nowhere a great gray bird came down, first a soundless shadow and then a somehow unreal though solid presence, big as a man, squatting in the grass before them. Catherine half-raised one hand, as if to point, then froze.

"Greetings, Roolf." The bird's voice was as soft and musical as that of the previous night's messenger, but Rolf thought this was a different bird; most of them looked much alike to him. The bird went on: "Strijeef of the Feathered Folk sends his greetings."

"Take mine to him, good messenger, if you will. What other news?"

"Only that, to the south of you, humans and powers are gathering still, of the East and of the West. It seems that both armies may follow yooou intooo the north."

"Are there any orders for me?"

"Prince Duncan sends you this word: I am to take what you are carrying, and fly on with it ahead, if you can tell me where to go with it; if Ardneh does not object."

Rolf thoughtfully fingered the pouch wherein the great jewel lay. "No. Tell the Prince the answer must still be no. If it seems I am about to be taken, then come to me if you can, and I will give you this. Not otherwise."

The bird was silent for a bit, then fixed enormous yellow eyes on Catherine. "I must take a report back on this one whooo travels with you."

"She does so by Ardneh's will. She is an enemy of the East, that much I am sure about. And a former neighbor of Duncan's, it would seem. Come, bird, the light is growing. Rest with us through the day; we can find some good place among these trees. We will talk. Then tomorrow night you can bear my answers back to Duncan."

A little later, when they were securely hidden in a

thicket, Rolf looked closely at the stunned face of Catherine, who had not said a word since the bird came down. With a rare full smile on his own face, he said: "Welcome. You see that you have reached the armies of the West."

V

Little Moment of Revenge

After speeding Rolf on his way with a final wave, Chup crouched down between Mewick and Loford on the little sheltered ledge they had scooped out of the side of the ravine. Looking to the southeast, he could see the Constable's force just coming into sight a kilometer away. Despite the distance, Chup thought that he could distinguish Charmian's long golden hair. An illusion, she would have it bound up for the ride. He told himself he should have killed her when he had the chance . . . Mewick was plucking at his sleeve, and motioning that it was time to move. Down in the bottom of the ravine, Chup mounted and followed the other six men remaining in the party, riding in a single file angling up the side of the ravine. Mewick was leading them to the northeast, at right angles to the course that Rolf had chosen.

About a dozen reptiles were in the sky, Chup noted as they reached the top of the slope and trotted toward the next ravine. The leatherwings were beginning to concentrate above the little Western force. Chup caught another glimpse of Abner's force, advancing steadily, beginning now to come into the broken country.

The chances of perpetrating an ambush seemed vanishingly small at the moment. To Loford, just ahead of him, Chup called: "What's in your bag of tricks, stout one?"

Mewick at the head of the file heard him, turned and called: "Let us see what we can find in our

arrow-bags first.'' And then he led them down one
ravine in a sudden dash toward the enemy column
that sent the reptiles speeding ahead to croak their
warnings, and then back up another, smaller, nar-
rower ravine, on a winding, reversing course that
took them out of sight of the reptiles. Mewick there-
upon abruptly called a halt, and with virtuosic gestures bade his men draw and nock arrows and aim
into the air. When the first reptiles came coasting
back over the hilltop close above, to discover what
had happened to the vanished subjects of their sur-
veillance, the ready volley brought down one and
winged another. While the flock was still recoiling
in noisy outrage from this ambush, Mewick led his
men on up the winding ravine at a headlong gallop,
once more unobserved by the foe. Following some
instinct of his own that seemed as accurate as aerial observation, he halted again suddenly, dismounted, and scrambled up a slope to peer through
grass at the top. Letting out a hissing noise of satisfaction, he once more pantomimed his wish for
archery, this time even correcting his men's angle of
aim, and then, with an unmistakable slashing gesture, bidding them loose their arrows blindly. Before the shafts could have fallen from the sky upon
any targets, Mewick was in the saddle again and
leading the retreat. There was a pained outcry from
somewhere below.

The little volley of arrows had fallen scattered
among and around the front of the enemy column,
and one of them had drawn blood. More important,
it stopped the enemy's forward progress for the
moment, and assured its somewhat slower and
more cautious movement in the future.

Mewick now led his men toward the north, for the
time being making no effort to do anything but keep
between the enemy and the course he wanted them
to think that Rolf was following.

The morning wore along uneventfully. The two
groups of mounted men made their way steadily

northward on parallel courses. Around the line of march the desert badlands reared up strange barren shapes of rock, among which smaller rocks lay jumbled and dry ravines lost their way.

Mewick somehow found a reasonably straight way through. Then suddenly he stopped, staring intently at the reptiles in the sky. "Demons of all the East!" he muttered fiercely. "But they are getting away from us. West! We must get west, and catch up with them!"

Riding hard, they topped a rise and caught sight of the enemy column moving away to the northwest, seemingly right on the trail of Rolf who had evidently not managed to shake the reptiles after all. Abner had maneuvered himself between the fugitives he was trying to overtake, and the annoying, elusive handful of men who were trying to delay him.

Mewick kept his men moving forward briskly. "Wizard?" he asked.

Loford, riding now in the middle of the file, was letting his mount find its own way, while his large blue eyes looked into distances that were not of earth or sky, and his fingers fumbled in a bag he had withdrawn from his pack. His gross body jiggled unheeded with the rapid ride. He took from the cloth bag a smaller bag of leather, curiously decorated in many colors, and from that in turn a length of sandy-colored twine, twisted into many strange knots. He rode on for some distance, fingering this absently, then suddenly seemed to come to himself, and with a throat-clearing got the attention of all the others.

"Hum. As the signs and powers now stand, the only thing of any consequence that I can manage successfully is to evoke a desert-elemental. But even at best to call one up will mean some difficulty and danger for us all. At worse—well things could get quite out of hand."

Mewick shook his head. "You had best try. Our

swords and arrows are too few, unless we can get between them and Rolf once more."

"I am wondering," Chup put in, "how strong a wizard they have with *them*. Not that our pudgy fellow here is easily overmatched, but the Constable of the East will surely be well attended in that regard."

"As to that," said Loford, unperturbed, "we will soon enough find out. Now let me do my work. No, keep moving. Just a little silence; I can raise an elemental as well as almost any other man, while I ride on beast-back if need be."

With fingers suddenly turned extremely skillful, he tilted the little leather bag so that there ran from it a thin stream of ordinary-looking sand, falling to be lost along the trail. Holding the bag in one hand while it slowly continued to spill, he used his other hand and his teeth to tug at certain places in the curiously knotted twine. One by one knots fell away and straightened out. Counting knots as they disappeared, Chup caught his breath. "We'll all be sandblasted to the bone," he muttered. But he made no real protest; heroic measures were called for.

Loford's art took quick effect. Looking to the northwest, beyond the enemy force, Chup watched the sandy land seem to shake out its dunes like wrinkles from a blanket, rising with the appearance of a single deep ocean swell as far as eye could see to right and left. Chup, who had seen similar things before, knew it was not in fact the whole earth lifting up, only surface sand raised by a great wave of wind, yet involuntarily he tried to brace his feet more firmly in the stirrups.

Reptiles chattered and shrieked alarm. From near the head of the distant Eastern mounted column, one tiny mounted figure detached itself, spurring with seeming confidence toward the oncoming wall of sand that here and there took on vague shapes of hands and jaws. It would be the Constable's wizard. The tiny man-figure raised its arms, and Chup heard Loford grunt as if he had received a blow. The stout magician turned his animal aside, slid awkwardly from the saddle, and sank down on one knee, eyes squinted shut, while his comrades reined to a halt around him.

"Ah, Ardneh," Loford groaned, "Ardneh, help! He means to turn what I have raised against us."

The galloping Eastern wizard seemed to be under no such strain as Loford suffered. Riding easily, he moved his outstretched arms forward and down toward the oncoming elemental; Chup, watching, had the impression of a tremendous quelling, quieting force. But it might almost have been the useless gesture of a child. The wavefront of wind and wind-blown earth poured on remorselessly and struck. For a moment or two there remained a tiny isle of calm, around the mounted Eastern magician, not much wider than his arms could stretch, in which air fell quiet and lifeless before his counterspell. But then he and his defended island vanished; the elemental rolled on unimpeded, reaching out monstrous half-living paws of sand and air for Abner and his fifty men.

With a cry of relief, Loford staggered to his feet. Then the elemental's peripheral winds and dust were beating on the Western men. Chup felt the sting and lash of sand, and the air was a sudden shriek around his ears. The bright sun, and his friends, were suddenly gone, concealed within the desert as it walked. When things cleared for a moment, he glimpsed the dense core of the elemental squatting some hundreds of meters to the northwest, right where Abner's force had been. Abner's force was still there, from the look of things. Out of the solid-looking clouds of raging sand came Eastern men individually, riding, staggering, crawling; and here and there fled blinded and demented animals. This elemental would not kill, at least not quickly and not often, but it would surely disable any human fighting force it settled on.

Chup cried out: "Ah, for a score of men to charge them now!" But to charge and fight in the heart of the storm would be to put oneself under the same disadvantage as the enemy, and he knew full well the impulse had to be restrained. Mewick instead used the time gained to best advantage by getting his few men once more between Rolf and the disorganized foe. The reptiles, hit harder than any land creatures by the elemental's blasts, were swept from the sky for the time being, and Mewick found a place against the steep side of a sheer jutting rock, where his men might hope to remain unobserved should the reptiles manage to come back, and from which they might sally out to sting the Constable again if and when he came on in pursuit of Rolf.

Chup huddled with the others between sheltering rocks, muffling his face with his cloak against the sand. Once more Loford groaned. "Now they too are getting help from greater powers," he muttered.

The wind died suddenly, rose again, then came and went in fitful gusts. Squinting into the sky above the enemy, Chup could see that the Eastern wizard had at last been able to call upon some effective force. The elemental was broken into a multitude of smaller whirlwinds, each of which raised a cloud of sand and dust, but which taken all together lacked the purpose and power that the single great creature had possessed. He could see, too, that Loford had not abandoned the struggle. The numerous whirlwinds danced around a common center, and seemed to be striving continually to reunite.

"The wind is no longer so bad we cannot walk or ride," Mewick shouted to his men, making himself heard above the shrieking air. "Let us see if we can strike another blow!"

Abner had lost two men to the elemental, one blinded permanently by sand, the other left crazed and unable to do more than whimper to himself. It was midday before he had his forces properly mar-

shalled again, the hopelessly wounded disposed of
and their riding-beasts and other useful property
distributed among the well. The wind was now no
worse than a bearable storm. He considered dividing his force, feeling reasonably confident that
there was no superior enemy body anywhere near,
but decided against it when his wizard assured him
that the winds must continue to decline.

The Constable cast a final look at his assembled
force (the woman Charmian, dressed like a soldier
and muffled against sand like the others, smiled
bravely and admiringly at him; well, he couldn't
have left her at the caravanserai, there was no telling
when he'd be able to go back) and got it moving
forward again. Scarcely had they gone a kilometer,
however, when there came a few more arrows down
upon them, from a hilltop close ahead. One more
man was hit. At the Constable's order forty cavalry
charged the hill with leveled lances, but its top was
now deserted, and behind it several ravines offered
concealment for a small force and the possibility of
further ambushes. The Constable's horn sounded a
recall.

Again they moved on to the northwest. The first
reptile able to return to the column, between disabling wind-blasts, reported flatter, grassier country ahead, into which the two fleeing Westerners
were making steady progress, while the seven
others remained between the fleeing two and Abner. The Constable consulted his weary wizard,
who confirmed him in his opinion that the two more
distant fugitives had the huge important gem with
them. The Constable ground his teeth and profaned
the names of demons in his anger. He felt by no
means certain of getting back the gem. Though the
long hours of a summer afternoon still lay ahead,
the sun had by now definitely passed its highest
point.

There now arrived a reptile-courier from the Emperor of the East himself, who was with his main

armies in the field a good many kilometers to the
south. The courier bore an answer to the Constable's urgent dispatch of the early morning, informing the court that an object had been stolen similar
to, but even larger than, that which had been used in
the unsuccessful attempt to neutralize Ardneh. The
answer from Ominor now was that the object was
certainly of great importance, and the Constable
must take personal command of the attempt to get it
back. Also that he must conduct his search to the
northwest—divination at the highest level gave assurance that the thing was being taken in that direction. Also, that reinforcements were being sent as
quickly as possible to the Constable's aid. The first
of these, a flight of a hundred additional reptiles,
began to arrive shortly after the courier.

The West, too, Abner thought sourly, would
doubtless be throwing in reinforcements, and there
would come a hundred more birds to harass him
through the night. As the reptiles came in, he sent
them to scour the country far ahead, to try to discover where the fugitives were heading.

Half an hour's steady forward progress followed,
before one of the scouting reptiles came screaming
that the small Western force was drawing up in a
line on a hilltop directly in their line of march.

"Seven men? I wish they would make such a
stand."

When he had got a little closer and could better
see the hill, he realized the Western maneuver was
not so foolish as it had sounded. The slope was very
wide from left to right, and too steep for mounted
men to charge up it at any speed in the loose sand.
Once more they would take casualties from arrows
and find the foe gone when they reached the top.
But to go clear around the hill would let the enemy
succeed in delaying them, without paying anything
for the privilege . . . Abner quickly decided to
spread his men out and charge the hill. He would
accept two or three casualties to inflict one; he

would be delayed little if at all; and there was always
the chance the fools would stand and fight.

The skirmish went about as he had expected, except that the Western arrows came down a little
more thickly than he had hoped, so Abner left four
men upon the slope. And when the crest was
reached, the foe was gone, except for one who lay in
the sand with the shaft of an Eastern arrow protrud-
ing from his head.

At any rate the country from here on was definitely flatter; the harassing enemy would have to
remain at a greater distance. He could see the six
riders on a distant rise, as if beckoning him to follow. Above them (at a safe altitude) many reptiles
were cawing loudly and circling in the sky; but his
wizard motioned in a slightly different direction,
and in that way Abner directed his troops.

The hours of light remaining were still long, but
inexorably growing shorter. Some of the reptiles
sent to scout far ahead of the two fugitives began to
return, saying they could find no settlements, no
buildings, nothing that looked as if it might be the
fugitives' goal. Grass grew tall and thick in that land,
the reptiles reported, and trees in ever-increasing
numbers. There were many places where the two-
legged beasts could go to earth once darkness had
fallen, and finding them again in the morning might
not be easy. How far ahead were the fugitives now?
Several kilometers. It was hard to say exactly; the
reptiles' horizontal-distance sense, like that of the
birds, was poor.

Abner moved his troops at a hard pace, though
both men and animals were weary. He had the feeling he was gaining. No more hills obtruded themselves to give the six skirmishers another place to
make a stand. They kept half a kilometer ahead of
Abner in the open country, and seemed for the time
being powerless to do more.

Just when it seemed that the day was going
reasonably well after all, there sprang up another

wind from dead ahead, erecting another wall of dust whose sudden creation bespoke the working of more Western magic. But this wind brought little pain to sore Eastern faces; it was far weaker (or perhaps more subtle) than the desert-elemental had been. This had been born in the sea of grass that lay ahead, beyond the desert. It did not blind and abrade with particles or threaten to kill with heat.

Abner's wizard was hard at work in his saddle once more, gesturing with a talisman of some kind in each hand. Whether he was having any success was hard to judge; the wind appeared about the same, able to do no obvious harm. The Constable tried to recall the characteristics of prairie-elementals, which he assumed this was. He seemed to remember that bleakness and tangled grass and natural wind were three components, but there was something else too, something he could not quite remember. His schooling in this branch of magic had been sketchy, and was now far in the past.

They had left the desert behind them, and were struggling through the first of the grasslands, when he remembered the most pertinent characteristic of prairie-elementals: distance itself.

His eyes told him what was happening, now that he thought to look closely for it. Beneath the feet of his riding-beast, and those of the other animals in his troop, the grassy land was elongating in the direction of their travel, like an optical illusion in reverse. Three steps forward were required to cover the real distance normally contained in two.

With a shout the Constable called his magician to his side, dragged the wretch from his saddle, and beat him half a dozen vicious blows with the flat of his sword. "Blunderer! Traitor! Could you not tell me what was happening? Or are you too thick-witted to be aware of it yourself?" He yearned to strike with the working edge of the blade, but was not ready to leave himself effectively wizardless in the face of the enemy.

"Ah, mercy, Lord!" the beaten wizard cried.
"There be powers against me here such as I have
never faced before."

Charmian had ridden forward from her place
near the rear of the little column, and seeing that
the Constable glanced at her but did not at once
order her back, was emboldened to take part. To the
unhappy wizard she said savagely: "One fat lout
from the provinces opposes you, a man I have met
before and know to be nearly devoid of skill, compared to what my Lord Constable's wizard should
possess. My Lord Constable is ill-served indeed."

"I tell you I am blameless," the magician cried. He
had fallen on his knees before the mounted Constable, while behind them the column halted.

"Who has defeated you? What mighty power?"
the Constable demanded. "If you cannot tell me
even that much, why should I not take you for a
traitor, or an imbecile incompetent?"

"I know not what or who!" The magician's eyes
were wild. "I knew not even that I was being beaten,
until your mighty Lordship struck at me, as—as
indeed I must be grateful for, that I was not slain out
of hand."

Charmian's expression had changed as she listened, and now she put out a hand to Abner. "Wait,
my good Lord, if it please you. There may be something to what this man says. There is one among our
enemies who is subtle and powerful enough to con-
found most wizards in this way."

"So." Abner's rage was quickly transformed into
calculation. He knew by now that Charmian was
intelligent, or rather that she could be when it
suited her; and she had come close to Ardneh in the
past. "What more can you tell me on this point?"

She looked at Abner with an apparent anxiety to
please. "Little enough right now, my Lord. Let me
talk with this fellow for a while, as we go on, and it
may be I can learn something worth your hearing."

"So be it." With a savage gesture Abner got the

stalled column moving again—two-thirds speed was better than none—and then, grimacing, he got paper from his saddlebag and reluctantly prepared to send a message asking Wood for help.

Charmian now had perfect reason for riding next to the wizard, and holding with him a lengthy whispered conversation of which no one else could hear a word.

"So, fellow," she began, in a tone remote and commanding. "I have saved you from the punishment your clumsiness merits. If you wish me to remain your friend, there is a simple thing you can do for me in return."

He looked at her with fear and calculation. "I am eternally in your debt, fair lady. What is there I can possibly do for you?"

"It might seem unimportant to my Lord the Constable, and I have not bothered him with it. But it is a meaningful matter to me." She began to explain.

She had not said much before the wizard was shaking his head, and holding up a finger to stop her speech. "No, no. If it were possible to cast a spell and bring down some disabling woe on those two fleeing from us, I would have done so long ere this. It was one of the first things the Constable asked of me, before taking the field in pursuit of them. But it cannot be done so simply. Conditions are not right in many ways—"

"I care little or nothing about harming the man," Charmian broke in. "It is the girl, Catherine, who betrayed me." Her voice dropped lower still, hate tightening it like some rack-rope in a dungeon. "It was she who got them to manhandle me. I saw her smirking, gloating, over her little moment of revenge . . . well, I mean to have the last laugh over her. I must and I will. Find me a way to give me my revenge upon that girl, and I will reward you well." She shifted her body in the saddle and saw his eyes go wandering over her, as if they had no choice but to do so when she willed it. "But fail to do so, and I will

tell the Constable that which will bring his full
wrath back upon you; it hangs balanced over your
head already, and needs but a gentle touch to bring
it down. I will say that it was not Ardneh at all who
defeated you, but some trivial power."

"It was Ardneh, or his equal. It must have been."
Charmian did not appear to have heard.

The magician—he was using no name at all at
present, a procedure not unheard of among those of
his calling—rode on in silence for a little time, siz-
ing up with sidelong looks the woman who rode
beside him, taking her measure in more ways than
one. "No, no," he said again. "From here there is no
way that I can visit on this fleeing servant girl the
tortures that you have in mind. We have no hair of
hers, or nail clippings, or even anything she
owned—hey? I thought not. Even a comparatively
mild curse would take—no, there is no way."

But Charmian was quick to catch him up. "Would
take what?"

The nameless magician evidently regretted starting to say whatever it was that he had left un-
finished. How could he have made such a clumsy
slip?

"Disagreeable fool, you are going to have to tell
me sooner or later."

Imagine a vast buried sea of power, into which a
man might hope to sink a secret well, not in safety,
but still with reasonable hope of not being caught in
a disaster, because he and a few others had managed to do it successfully a few times in the past.
The Nameless One pondered briefly and fatalisti-
cally the secret syllables of a Name forbidden to be
spoken. Wood knew that name, and Ominor of
course, and four or five others in the highest coun-
cils of the East. It was seldom even alluded to—the
Nameless One had heard Wood do so only once, on
the day of Ardneh's visit to the capital.

Charmian prodded him: "It would seem to be a
worthless power, or whatever it is, if it cannot be

used." And again: "Remember, I meant what I said, both my promise and my threat."

The Nameless One believed her. "All right, then. We will see. I will try what can be tried."

Throughout the remainder of the day, the Constable gained upon his prey, but not enough. As sunset came, the wind abated and the prairie-elemental died; but the night belonged to the West, and Abner reluctantly gave orders to make camp and set a vigilant guard.

VI

Ardneh

———————————◆◆◆◆———————————

Rolf was saying: "You told me yourself that your Offshore man is likely wedded by now to someone else. What does it matter, then, if you should come and sit by me?

It was morning again, the second since their flight had begun. The bird had gone into hiding for the day in a nearby tree, where he—or she, Rolf was not sure—was now practically invisible. Since talking with the bird, Catherine and Rolf had slept a little, and had drunk their fill of fresh running water.

She looked at him now with what was almost a smile. "Is it some military matter you wish to discuss?" Catherine had been kneeling on the stream's grassy bank trying to see her face in the water below. The swelling on her cheekbone had gone down, but the discoloration was if anything worse than before, mottling from purple into green.

"Well . . ." He spread his hands. "We could begin with military secrets. You are at least four meters away, and to shout them across such a space would put them in danger of being overheard by the enemy." He looked up and around him with a great show of wariness. Catherine almost laughed.

They were in a little grove cut through by the stream. Looking out of the shade of the trees Rolf could see in all directions, fields and gentle hills of grass dotted here and there with other copses or single trees. It might be the patchy remnants of a receding forest or the struggling outposts of a new one.

Rolf sat with his back against a fallen trunk, facing across the stream, which was here only six or eight meters wide, and very shallow. With his right hand he patted the smooth grass beside him, indicating to Catherine where she was invited to sit.

She had given up trying to study her face in the water, but as yet she came no closer. "I do not know, sir, whether I should. Still, I suppose you are now my commanding officer, and if I flout your orders I am liable to find myself in some military court."

A cloud of irritation passed over his face. "No, don't joke about that. Giving orders, I mean." She sat back with her feet tucked under her, looking at him steadily. "I mean, I have seen people I knew executed by military courts. I'm sorry, I didn't mean to squelch a joke. You must have had few chances for them, since . . . when were you taken by the East?"

"A lifetime ago." No longer close to laughing, she got up slowly, and with her hands rubbed her bare arms as if she were peeling, scraping, something off. "But let's not talk about that now. I wish this stream were deep enough to swim and soak in it." Her servant's dress was stained, as were Rolf's clothes, with travel and hard usage, and her bound-up brown hair was dull with dust. But she looked less tired by far than she had before their flight.

"We could look for a deeper place," he said. "I would enjoy a swim myself, I think." He felt a little pulse begin, inside his head.

"Leave these trees, in daylight?"

"I meant tonight. At dusk."

She came nearer then, though not quite as near as his patting hand had indicated, and sat down. Her eyes flicked at him, unreadably; at nineteen he had long since given up trying to understand women.

He said: "I should never have mentioned that man you were to wed."

"No. I am thinking only of the girl I was, and how I have been changed. How when I was young I flirted and laughed and teased."

"When you were young? What are you now, about seventeen?"

"Two years ago I was fifteen, I think. But now I am no longer young."

"So, you are really such an old woman." Now his voice was growing more soft and tender. "Then you must be a fit companion for an old man like myself." And somehow he had traversed the little distance that had been between them, and his fingers had begun a gentle stroking of her bare arm, up to the coarse slave's-cloth at the shoulder.

Her look seemed to say to him that his behavior was far from being unendurable; that, perhaps, if it went on a little longer it might begin to give her pleasure. His arm would have needed less encouragement than that to start unhurriedly going around her. It had always seemed to Rolf something of a wonder how this hard and angular limb of his always managed to adapt itself so neatly and exactly to the soft job of girl-holding. This one was certainly a soft girl now, regardless of how lean and strong she had appeared only a little while ago. Now in response to a firm pressure of his fingers on her cheek (safely below the blackened eye) her face turned round to his more fully. He found her lips.

Her smooth face rubbed willingly under his straggly beard. Time passed, then seemed about to be forgotten. Now he would kiss tenderly the swelling on her cheekbone, before he began a line of kisses moving down her throat.

Now, what was this upon her skin?

What had happened—

What —

With an outcry Rolf sprang to his feet and backed away, stumbling and almost falling in his haste. He grabbed up his sword and half-drew it from its sheath before he was aware of doing so, and when he became aware he scarce knew whether to finish pulling out the blade or push it back.

Before him now, and lately enfolded most tenderly in his arms, was one of the most hideous human shapes it had ever been his ill fortune to behold. What had been Catherine's healthy young face had altered while he kissed it to the visage of a withered, snaggle-toothed, misshapen crone. Even where he now stood, some meters distant, he thought he could still taste the pestilent breath. Under stiff, dirt-colored hair, tied up just as the young girl's had been, were the face and neck of an unrecognizable old woman, skin wrinkled as a rag, dotted with warts and here and there a whisker. The strong smooth arms that Rolf had felt about his neck were shrunken now to quivers of loose skin in which bones slid like crooked arrows. The breathing that had moved young breasts against him now had altered to a scraping wheeze, coming from a body as shapeless as the dress that covered it.

The old woman staggered to her feet, groping before her with fingers gnarled like roots. Her features worked, but her face was so distorted by age and disease that Rolf could not for a moment guess whether it was terror, anger, or laughter that moved her now.

Moving like some crippled sleepwalker, she tottered toward him on the brink of the grassy bank. "Rolf?" she cawed out the one word, in something like a reptile's voice, and then her figure seemed to blur, and down she fell on hands and knees.

Later he could not estimate how long he had stood there, rubbing his eyes, trying to see the figure before him clearly once again. In time he discovered that the blurring was not in his eyes, but in the female shape before them. Then all at once she was as she had been before he took her in his arms; healthy and young, the purplish-green bruise upon her cheek, vital brown hair struggling to escape the tie that bound it up. It was Catherine on her hands and knees, her face convulsed in terror. "Rolf?" she cried out once again, this time in her own voice, and he threw down his sword and fell on his knees beside her.

She covered her face with her hands, until he pulled them away gently. Her whisper was still terrified: "How do you see me now?"

He put out a hand to caress her, but sudden suspicion made him draw it back. "As a girl. As you were when we first met."

"Thank all the powers of the West. Then she could not make it permanent . . . why do you still look at me so? What *do* you see?"

Shaken, he blurted clumsily: "I see a girl. But how do I know which is your true shape, this one or the other? What kind of magic is this?"

"What kind of magic? *Hers*, the evil woman's . . . she has found some way to do this foul thing to me. I know it." Now the first immensity of Catherine's terror was gone, but tears were standing in her eyes. "I heard it from her and others, that never in my life should I escape her. The Lady Demon, Charmian."

Gazing at the young form before him, Rolf suddenly could no longer believe that it might be a lie, the product of some Eastern enchantment. Catherine had none of Charmian's glamor; her youth and health was marked with human awkwardness and imperfection. She was too complete and varied to be unreal. He said, reassuringly: "There are Western wizards who can deal with any spell."

"Hold me," she whispered, and he took her in his arms again. For a while he comforted, he soothed, and all was well. Once more he kissed the bruised cheekbone, which this time did not change. And then, as his caresses ceased to be meant as comforting, he saw the first sagging wrinkle appear upon her cheek.

This time he did not retreat so rapidly or so far, but still he let her go. This time he watched the progress of the cycle with compassion, as Catherine passed through decrepit ugliness and back to youth again. Then they were silent for a little while, looking at each other like grave children.

"It is when I embrace you as a man with a woman that it happens," he said at last. And she nodded, but made no other move. A long time passed before she spoke at all.

Near sundown, as Rolf awoke from a fitful sleep and began to prepare for another night of travel, he saw a great swarm of reptiles taking shelter for the night in a grove about a kilometer to the southeast. Rolf could see no Eastern ground forces, but they must be near; the reptiles would need at least a few human defenders to survive the night if they were discovered by the Feathered Folk.

With the first true darkness, the bird awoke, and came to perch briefly on Rolf's hospitably leveled forearm, settling with a surprising spread of soft, balancing wings; it weighed no more than a small child. Pointing south with his free hand, Rolf said: "It is good we did not rest in that grove instead, for there the trees have just filled up with leather."

"Hooo! Then I must go quickly and gather my people here."

"I have some words for you to carry to Duncan, also. Some Eastern magic has been worked upon us." While Catherine stood by listening, he told the bird in brief what had happened.

"Carry word also," Catherine added, "that our riding-beasts are failing. One is too far gone to be ridden, I think, and the other not much better."

Rolf went to inspect the animals himself, but had to agree that Catherine was right. The bird took thought, and then offered: "Let them gooo free. I will send birds tonight to ride and goad them far from here, so if the East should find them tomorrow they will be misled."

The few belongings they had, weapons and cloaks and a small store of food, made no great burden. With compact bundles on their backs, Rolf and

Catherine waved goodby to the bird and stepped off once more to the northwest, at first following the stream closely. There would be no looking for bathing-spots tonight, not with the enemy only a kilometer away. He and Catherine managed to cover about fifteen kilometers before dawn. During the night they saw no more birds; probably all who could fly had been mustered for an attack on the roosting reptile horde.

There was no difficulty on the next morning—or on the next, after another uneventful night of walking—about finding places in which to hide. The country through which they traveled was gradually becoming more thickly wooded, though still the long grass was dominant. The land also grew hillier, and was threaded at frequent intervals with small streams which ended any remaining concern about finding water. Catherine got her bath at last, in privacy.

"You can take a little walk now, Rolf. I'll catch up when I'm through."

"What's the matter? Hey, why pull away?"

She looked at him steadily and pulled away even a little farther. "How can you ask that?"

"Well, but the curse may have expired by this time."

"Or it may have grown more powerful. I'll not risk it again. It was easy enough for you, you didn't have to feel your own body . . . changing. Don't try to touch me."

And he had to admit, with an unwilling sigh, that she was right.

Several more nights of travel passed without notable incident. Nightly a bird came to them, bringing news of how the rival armies had maneuvered the day before. Duncan, the birds reported, was receiving from his wizards ever-stronger omens of the importance of Ardneh to the West, and of Rolf's mission for Ardneh. The Prince had dispatched a cavalry force to overtake Rolf and act as his escort to wherever Ardneh wanted him to go. But the Western cavalry detailed for the job had been intercepted by strong Eastern patrols, who were also converging upon the area, and forced to fight. John Ominor was now thought to have taken direct command of the main Eastern army in the field, though if so he was careful to stay hidden in his tent at night, out of sight of birds.

On another night, one of drizzling rain, Rolf and Catherine came to a stream wider than any they had met so far. Squinting into the murky dark, Rolf found he could not tell if the far bank was thirty meters distant or three hundred. At the moment no bird was with them to act as guide. The river flowed roughly to the north, but as soon as Rolf began to follow its bank in that direction a sudden hard feeling of wrongness, almost a sickness, came over him. When he stopped, the malaise subsided, only to return full force when he would have gone on again. Catherine felt nothing, but he could scarcely walk. Only when he reversed himself and followed the stream south did the sensation leave him. His puzzlement ended a hundred meters upstream, where what he first took to be a very odd-shaped stone in his path revealed itself on examination to be one end of a large metal object, almost completely buried.

Since Ardneh had apparently led them to it, he and Catherine set to work with knife and hatchet to dig the thing out of the hardened earth. They had not got far before they realized they were uncovering a small boat, made of Old World metal, uncorrupted by whatever ages it had lain under the ground. In an hour or so they had the craft dug out; it proved to be practically undamaged and perfectly usable, of a handy size for two passengers. Oars or paddles there were none, but a little groping in the dark turned up a couple of branches suitable for poles if the water were not too deep. Rolf took it for granted that his proper course was still to the north, downstream. They loaded their little gear into the boat and put out into the river, finding it fairly swift and shallow. Before dawn they had made, while resting their feet, several more kilometers toward their still unknown goal.

That day they spent mostly in the boat, tied up to the shore under a sheltering overhang of bushes. For the first time in days Rolf spotted a reptile; but the enemy was cruising deep in the remote southern sky, and there was no reason to think it had seen them. Toward evening Rolf took a couple of fish with a whittled spear, and at sunset Catherine cooked them over a small fire. The food in their packs was beginning to run low.

That night, drifting north again over moonlit water, Rolf felt the conviction begin to grow in him that he was nearing the end of his journey.

The river wound its way north among the grassy hills of a land that seemed utterly empty of intelligent life. Near the end of their second night on the water they drifted past the mouth of a tributary creek, and Rolf obeying a sudden powerful impulse turned the boat into it. Poling the boat upstream was difficult, and the creek soon became so shallow that the boat scraped bottom frequently. Rolf and Catherine emptied it of their belongings and let it drift free, back to the larger stream that would carry it away from their path.

By now it was light enough for reptiles to be out, but Rolf decided to push on. Brush growing along the watercourse offered some concealment, and he had the sense that some conclusion was imminent, the feeling that it would not greatly matter if some reptile saw them now. Suspiciously he tried to analyze this feeling, and decided that it came from Ardneh and was to be trusted.

The water offered a path in which they would leave no trail. They waded on up the stream, which was only four or five meters wide here and not much more than ankle-deep.

"Why should the water be so cold?" Catherine asked him. Rolf frowned, realizing that she was right; the land was deep in summer, and such a little stream did not have depths to hold a chill. Unless it was the outflow of some deep lake . . .

A final meandering of the stream between its gentle banks brought them round a little hill, and he understood. The creek vanished unexpectedly into a hillside hole, a tunnel-mouth with a ledge at one side just above the water level.

He stood with Catherine before the tunnel-mouth for a little time, and then said: "This is where we are to go." He felt her shiver beside him; chill air emerging from some underground depth, flowed almost imperceptibly around them, and their breaths steamed despite the growing radiance of the rising sun. "Come," he said, and loosened his sword in its scabbard and moved forward. Here the water narrowed and deepened quickly and he climbed out of it to take the dry ledge that emerged from the hillside beside the stream.

Clay and dank limestone folded them about, and as they proceeded the tunnel gradually grew darker. It was far too regular to be natural, and marks showed of the hand tools that had shaped its surface.

"A mine," said Catherine. "I have never been in one before."

"Nor I. But you are right, it must be a mine." Perhaps, Rolf thought, diggers after some useful metal had by accident run into an underground vein of water, and had dug this channel for it to keep their works from being flooded. That must have been long ago, for the creek bed outside looked as old as any other on the prairie.

The passage curved, but not into the blinding darkness that Rolf had expected. Ahead, it was joined by a vertical shaft, letting in the light of day from what must be a hilltop some meters overhead. Looking up through the rough shaft when he reached it, Rolf beheld a small circle of blue sky, fringed with stirring grass.

"Look," urged Catherine, pointing downward. Half-embedded in the undisturbed clay beneath their feet were rusted lumps of metal that must once have been tools.

Rolf started to say something, then fell silent. He waited, listening, then moved silently to look back down the passage in the direction they had come. It might have been a drop of water that he had heard, falling from the wet stone and clay of the tunnel's roof. After a moment he shook his head, returned to where Catherine stood with a nocked arrow in her bow, and beckoned her to follow him. Their journey's end was near, but they had not reached it yet.

"What are we do to here?" she whispered at his back, but he did not know and did not answer. Beyond the vertical shaft, the horizontal one continued, into truly growing darkness.

Going slowly to let his eyes adjust to deepening gloom, Rolf edged forward, his feet just above the steady murmur of the stream. Here was where the stream gushed into the tunnel, from an indistinguishable crevice at one side. Not a dozen meters farther on, with the floor of the tunnel now completely dry, the miners' ancient work abruptly broke off. More crumbling tools lay, as if dropped while in use, against the tunnel's deepest face, and high in that face a hole remained, leading to a deeper darkness. The ancient diggers might have broken through, but had not entered whatever chamber lay beyond, for the hole was not big enough . . .

The aperture flamed abruptly, with cold, clear light. Catherine let out a little cry and raised her bow. Rolf started, but in the next moment felt relief. He knew Old World illumination when he saw it, hard and bright and steadier than any flame. He had seen it before, and then as now Ardneh had been his guide.

He reassured Catherine, and together they

peered into the hole. It opened into a simple room about five meters square, with gray smooth walls and flat panels in the ceiling from which the cold light flowed tirelessly. A closed door stood in the opposite wall.

Groping among the fallen miners' tools, Rolf found the head of a pickaxe that was not too corroded to be effective, and with it he worked at enlarging the hole the miners had abandoned. Maybe the Old World lights had flashed for them as well, and they had chosen to drop their tools and run, not coming back.

Catherine worked at his side, clearing away lumps of rock and clay and smooth gray paneling as he broke them loose. The hole was soon enlarged enough for them to squeeze through. The floor was of the same gray stuff as the walls. Scattered on the floor and on a few shelves along one wall were a number of metallic-looking boxes, neatly marked with words in a language neither Rolf nor Catherine could read. The room and its contents were vastly better-preserved than the less ancient miners' tools had been, but even here Time had begun to have his way. From one spot on the ceiling a waxy-looking icicle depended, and Rolf on touching it found that it was rock, with a slow drop of ground water gathering on its tip, and a small rocky stalagmite building on the floor beneath. He shivered suddenly in the chill cave air, with a sudden sense of what time might mean.

The door leading out of the room tried to stay shut when he twisted at its handle and shoved against it with a shoulder, but then it yielded with a sudden rasp. The passage beyond the door was revealed abruptly as its ceiling panels sprang to glowing life.

"Come," said Rolf, as Catherine hung back again. "I tell you it is all right. This is where we are to be."

They moved on through the new passage in the direction that seemed right to Rolf, passing through other corridors and chambers. The sound of the stream in the tunnel was lost somewhere behind them. In time they reached a room where the air was warm and their breath no longer steamed.

Time had hardly entered here as yet. There were many metal cabinets and racks, seeming perfectly preserved, filled with equipment Rolf could not begin to guess the purpose of, but which yet gave him an impression of a high degree of organization.

On the most prominent panel at one end of the room stood bold symbols that he could not read, but which he recognized as having the look of certain Old World writings that he had seen before:

AUTOMATIC RESTORATION DIRECTOR—
NATIONAL EXECUTIVE HEADQUARTERS

"Rolf."

The voice was pleasant, masculine but not heavily so. It came from somewhere in the cabinetry behind the lettering. Rolf did not even start at the sound, but only raised his eyes; he knew at once that it was Ardneh calling him. Catherine had almost literally jumped with surprise, and now stood poised as if to flee; but she waited with her eyes on Rolf.

Rolf said: "Ardneh?", half expecting a figure to materialize. But there were only the metallic-looking cabinets, from one of which the voice of Ardneh issued again.

"Do not fear me, Catherine. Do not fear, Rolf; for years you and I have known each other, dimly, but in trust."

"I do not fear you, Ardneh, no," said Rolf. He held out a hand, and Catherine came slowly to his side. "You can show yourself, Ardneh, and we will not be afraid."

"I have no flesh to show you, Rolf. Nor am I of pure energy, like an elemental or a djinn. But I am of the West, and I need your help."

"That is why we are here." Rolf paused. "Are you then like Elephant that I once knew, some war machine of the Old World? But no, you have life and thought, where Elephant was mindless as a sword."

"You are partly right," said Ardneh's voice. "I am, or was, what you call a machine, and made by men of the Old World. But I was not made to fight a war, I was made to restore a peace. And for a long time I have, as you say, had life and thought."

Rolf turned around. "Where are you, then?"

"All around you. Each shelf and cabinet contains some part of me. As you see, I depend heavily on Old World technology, and it is because of your natural talent in such matters that I chose you and brought you here. The object you have brought me is important, but your own presence, Rolf and Catherine, is equally so."

Rolf put his hand on the pouch he carried. Ardneh said: "Bring what you call the gem along the path I will now show you. There is a test that must be made before my plans go further."

The lights in the room dimmed abruptly, but brightened beyond a doorway, in one external corridor. As Rolf and Catherine entered this corridor and followed it, the brightening of the lights moved on ahead of them, from one ceiling panel to another. After many winding passages, interspersed here and there with descending stairs, they entered another room, larger than that where Ardneh had first spoken and crowded with a number of strange devices. Into one of these, a simple-looking crystal-line case surrounded by a number of heavy metal rings, Ardneh told Rolf to drop the gem.

"And now leave this room," said Ardneh's voice, this time from a wall. "The test had better be made without human beings present." Leaving the chamber with Catherine, Rolf noticed doors as thick as castle walls, sliding from concealment to seal the passage behind them. Once more the overhead light danced on, leading them back to the room in which Ardneh had first spoken.

"Sit down, if you wish," Ardneh said when they were there again; and they seated themselves on the floor. "There is much I must tell you, for it is going to be necessary for you to tell others the truth about me; more than I dare now explain in the world outside these chambers, but which must be explained before many more days have passed.

"I was built by war-planners of the Old World, as part of a system of defense. But not as a destructive device. My oldest purpose is to defend mankind, and so I am of the West today, though there was no East or West when I was built. My basic nature is peaceful, so it has taken me long to develop weapons of my own to enter battle. The object you have brought me will add to the physical strength I can exert, if the test I am now conducting has a favorable result. More of that later.

"My builders meant their defense system to save the world, and in a sense it did. But they called on powers they did not fully understand and could not wholly control, and in saving the world they changed it, so drastically that their civilization could not survive. This was the great Change of which humans still speak, and it divided the Old World from the new.

"As I will show you soon, the world was changed by another machine, or rather by a part of me that has long since done its work and been dismantled. The part of me that still exists, was created to end the Change when the time was ripe. The builders did not really expect that the changes in the world wrought by their defenses would be so great that I would be needed, but they doubted and feared enough to make me and to put the powers of restoration under my control if they should be needed. They thought that fifty thousand years must pass before the proper time for restoration came. But only now has it arrived. The odds for the survival of mankind, if the restoration is accomplished in this year, in this month, are better than they have been at any time since the Change, or are likely to be in the estimable future."

Rolf asked: "And when this restoration you speak of is made, will it destroy the East?"

"I hope it will."

"Then let us restore the Old World, if you think that we of the West can live in it."

Ardneh seemed to ignore his advice, and Rolf had the uncomfortable feeling that he had been talking of things he knew nothing about.

Silently the overhead lights once more began their dance, leading them back to the room wherein they had left the mysterious gem. The heavy doors had reopened, and Rolf and Catherine entered to stare at the case in which they had left the ebon sphere. The sphere had been replaced by, or transformed into, a pearly, weightless-looking ball of light of about the same size. Looking at it, Rolf had the impression of effortless, tremendous power.

"It is what I thought it was," Ardneh's voice explained. "And my plans can now go forward."

"What?" Catherine whispered, staring in fascination.

"What a technologist of the Old World would have called the magnetohydrodynamic core of a hydrogen-fusion power lamp. From it I can draw renewed power, which is very important. Also important is what it shows. The fact that I have been able to change it from a gem back into what it was in the Old World, is a sure proof that the Change is weakening; that the restoration can be made."

Rolf sighed. "Ardneh, there is still much of this we do not understand. And you say it is necessary that we do so."

"Again, follow the lights. Watch and listen for a little while and then there will be time for food and rest."

This time they were led along yet another branching of the passageways, and to a still lower level. With every minute the buried complex housing Ardneh was revealed as larger, and there was no reason to think they had seen it all as yet.

In a room that must have been far below the level
of the outside ground, but where the air was fresh
and dry and comfortably warm, were couches covered in some leather-like substance that creaked
and crackled with age when Rolf and Catherine lay
down, but did not crumble. Above each couch and
pointed at its head were clustered metal rods, suspended from somewhere in the obscurity above the
lights.

The lights dimmed. "Now you will sleep," said
Ardneh. And so it was.

To Rolf there soon came a dream, so clear and
methodical a dream that he knew it was not natural.
Although he knew he was dreaming, he did not waken. He was drifting, no more than a disembodied
viewpoint, watching people who he somehow knew
were of the Old World. They were strangely dressed,
and spoke to one another in a tongue unknown to
Rolf, as they went about tasks that he at first found
completely incomprehensible. Then he saw that
they were pouring lakes into buried caverns, lakes
not of water but seemingly of sparkling, coruscating
liquid light.

Ardneh's voice, also bodiless, said: "Rolf, those
lakes were one attempt to prevent the Old World
from destroying itself, by strengthening the powers
of life. I was another attempt."

"I know what those lakes of life were like, Ardneh,
for I saw one spilled in the Black Mountains. Is there
one that Duncan can make use of, to restore his men
fallen in battle?"

"I think there are no more such lakes left in the
whole world, Rolf. Watch, now. This dream that you
see is something made by some leaders of the Old
World, to show other folk of that time how well they
were to be protected against war."

And Rolf, in the strange embrace of the bed which
he no longer felt, settled himself to watch the
dream. With only partial comprehension, despite
Ardneh's occasionally interjected words of expla-

nation, he watched as in scene after scene strangely-uniformed men and women built, armed, tested and concealed long finned cylinders, which Ardneh explained were rocket-driven missiles. Missiles were carried in strange craft moving hidden under the seas, were secreted in underground silos, were hung soaring in patient readiness so high above the ground that great earth itself became nothing but a ball. Small missiles intended to destroy large missiles were made in great numbers also, and one scene showed racks of these defensive weapons that swung out quickly from an artificial hillside.

Next, interspersed with views of men and women laboring at tasks even harder to understand, Rolf watched workers assembling the multitudinous cabinets of Ardneh in his cave. Or at least in some deep shelter. Rolf could not really recognize the uninhabited shelter in which he knew his sleeping body lay. Nor did the countryside around the site in the Old World much resemble that of Rolf's time, except that there were very few people in either.

"What are those things, Ardneh?"

"They are called heat-exchangers. They are sunk deep into the earth and draw power from it. Through the ages when all atomic devices were inoperative, I drew power from the heat-exchangers, and I draw it still. And now, Rolf, Catherine, behold the last days of the Old World, and its changing. First, what those who made me foresaw might happen; next, what actually did happen, as I later pieced it together."

Now the dream unrolling before Rolf with vivid precision no longer showed perfectly lifelike people and events, but instead what seemed to be a series of drawings that moved and spoke in close imitation of life. They were marvelous drawings, such as no artist known to Rolf could have fashioned. But they were lifeless nonetheless.

Rolf saw in this bloodless world of moving drawings how the huge missiles were fired in sudden salvos, taking flight from their many places of concealment. In swarms and clouds they leaped up high, ranged around the globe of earth, and fell again. As their blunt heads detached and multiplied themselves, down-curving toward their targets, the small missiles sprang up to meet them, shooting like darts from hidden defensive nests. When an offensive missile passed in killing range of a defender, a blast seared the upper air, and both were gone.

But the attack was too heavy; destructive devices from halfway around the world were falling upon the helpless-looking cities of Ardneh's builders. Only seconds remained before disaster. At once, the Ardneh portrayed in the moving drawings was shown fully alerted. To him—to it, rather, there was no sign that this Ardneh was intended to be, or thought to be, alive—was passed control of the ultimate defense.

With the help of Ardneh and the Old World dream machine Rolf was able to comprehend that this defense was in the nature of an experiment, involving the use of forces that must engulf the entire planet once they were unleashed, that were feared by some to be irreversible. They were newly-discovered forces that had never been tested and would not be tested now if destruction were not certain otherwise. The ultimate defense against atomic attack worked by robbing certain types of energy from certain atomic and subatomic configurations of matter, making the fusion or fission of nuclei enormously less likely.

A quick flicker in the drawings showed a subtle wave of change spreading out from the Ardneh-machine's emplacement, passing over the threatened cities of the homeland moments before the enemy's missiles struck within them. No murderous blasts erupted; the impacting warheads did no more damage than so many catapulted rocks.

What had happened to the enemy country was not apparent, but suddenly things at home were tranquil once again. A stylized drawing-man reached to touch one of Ardneh's control panels, and with the neatness of a folding parasol the protective change that Ardneh had thrown out was folded up, withdrawn, undone.

"So much for the plan," said Ardneh's voice, in present time. "And now behold what truly happened, at the changing of the world."

The visionary narrative of attack and defense began over again, with little change at first in the substance of the story. Again the offensive missiles came from around the world, launched in greater numbers and with more deceptive aids than could be dealt with by the conventional defense of short-range countermissiles. The Ardneh-machine was alerted in the first minutes of the great war, while the enemy attack was still no more than a network of trajectories in space, perceived and plotted by the defenders. While destruction was still minutes away, the counterattack was launched; whether Ardneh succeeded or failed, it seemed that the enemy must die.

Now disaster was only seconds away from most of the major cities of the land. The part of Ardneh that had been built to change the world was empowered to act, and it functioned as it had been made to do. It laid hold upon the matter within itself and pulled its energies into a new shape, beginning a Change that spread through the substance of the earth like cracks through shattering glass. A round wave-front of Change sprang out with the speed of light from Ardneh's buried site. But the setting in motion of the ultimate defense had taken a few seconds longer than anticipated. One enemy missile fell just before the wave-front reached it and exploded with full force beside a populous city, ending uncountable lives in the blinking of an eye. Other intercontinental weapons, falling like hail a few seconds later, failed to explode.

Meanwhile, on the other side of the world, surprise; the enemy was employing the same kind of an ultimate defense. But theirs was not controlled by any device as sophisticated as Ardneh, and their simpler mechanisms were never to become alive. This Rolf understood as in a dream, knowing it was so without knowing how he knew. But the enemy defenses also worked. A wave of Change springing from the other side of the world met that generated by Ardneh, and the fabric of the planet was altered more powerfully than anyone had expected.

Those few missiles that fell before the Change exploded, and the vast number that fell afterward were rendered practically harmless. One missile, however, to which Rolf's attention was now silently directed, was caught precisely in mid-explosion by the wavefront emanating from Ardneh. The fireball, the blooming nuclear blast, had just been born and it was not extinguished but neither did it follow the normal course of the explosions that had preceded it. It did not fade, but changed in shape, ran through a spectrum of colors and back again, and writhed up toward the sky as if with agonizing effort. Rolf knew that he was watching a kind of birth, and one of terrible importance.

With the passing of the wave of Change, Ardneh himself immediately began his first stirrings toward life, as did many other formerly inert components of the world.

But neither Ardneh nor any of the others accepted life as savagely, exultantly, as this.

VII

Orcus

———————◆—◆—◆———————

That writhing into a furious life, begun amid a violence beyond the capability of any human being to understand, was the earliest memory of the being who would later be named Orcus, later called Lord of Lords and Emperor of all the East. His earliest memory was recorded thousands of years before John Ominor was born, thousands of years before humanity lay divided into the two camps called East and West.

For a few thousand years after his violent birth, the being who would later be known as Orcus wandered in the desert places of the earth, avoiding humans, avoiding distraction as much as possible while he groped his way toward full sentience. Child of the awesome old technology and the marvelous new magic that had begun with the Change, his substance was only partially subject to the laws of matter.

There were others more or less like him now in the world, though none so terrible of birth or power. Quickly men began to forget their technology, maimed as it was by the Change; almost from the moment of the Change they were speaking of the Old World and the New, and taking up the newly opened possibilities of magic to help them finish their aborted war. Since the Change it could scarcely be said that anything was lifeless; powers that before had been only potentialities now responded readily to the wish, the incantation, were

motivated and controlled by the dream-like logic of
the wizard's world.

Humans grew aware of the existence of the being
who would be Orcus, and in their dogged search for
magical power they tried to devise means to control
him. These efforts were annoying to him, in his
growing self-awareness; to avoid them, when they
became persistent, he wandered away from earth.
Half-immune to the laws of physics and chemistry
as the Old World had known them, he drifted without sustenance and almost without effort outward
to the moon, where what had been human colonies
were now dead and deserted, casualties of war and
the failure of technology. Above the cratered surface
Orcus drifted, watching, beginning to think, as the
strange bubble-houses that had sheltered the humans decayed and burst in silence. All around,
soft-looking mountains two thousand thousand
times as old as humankind looked down, unchang-
ing and indifferent.

Orcus was beginning to think, and to feel sharp
emotions, and to be intensely aware of the world
and of himself. He began also to fear the empty
moon, and the soft deep beyond, that by its immensity made him feel that he was shrinking steadily.
Slowly through the solar winds of space he turned,
willing himself to begin the long drift back to earth.
He realized now that there, and perhaps nowhere
else, he was a giant.

Now as he approached the earth again he saw
humanity clearly, and began to understand and
loathe them. A new generation of sorcerers had de-
veloped in his absence, men and women of greater
magical skill and greater arrogance. These became
aware of the demon who would be Orcus, and when
they glimpsed his power they tried with fear and
greed to summon him and master him. But their
nets of magic burst and tore around him as he
moved.

Long and slow and difficult was the groping of the
demon to his full sentience and identity. Despite his
hatred of the wizards' race his own development
followed the same general direction as theirs, under
requirements imposed by the mental potentialities
of the home planet they shared. The ways of Orcus'
thought were not unlike those of the men he hated,
not when compared to others that he had dimly
sensed in the great deeps beyond the frightening
moon. (Never would he leave earth's air again.)

Orcus moved over the earth and looked at the life
upon it, with a hate and pointless envy that no man
or woman could match. In himself he was the East,
before the East had come to be. Men were building
new civilizations now; most of the Old World and its
technology lay buried and forgotten (unknown to
men and demons, Ardneh too was now living, thinking, waiting.) And he who would be Orcus became
aware now of others who were somewhat like himself, though smaller. These were demons and pro-
todemons born from sunlike fires as he had been,
but from comparatively minor acts of violence
crossed by the wave of change. None of these others
could begin to match his strength, and he cowed
them when he met them, never questioning his own
urge to dominate. Two other demons, who might in
time have grown great enough to challenge him
successfully, he met separately and slew. His struggle with one of these lasted for nearly a thousand
years, and nearly depopulated one of the earth's
smaller continents of human and animal life, before
he-who-would-be-Orcus managed to reach and
snuff out the hidden life of his opponent.

Shortly after that age-long struggle he received
his name. When he had made himself undisputed
king of the demonic powers of the world, and therefore the chief enemy of most of the human race,
magicians began to call him Orcus, after some
demon-lord of ancient Old World legend. (Had there
in fact been Old World demons, too? And was this

Changing from whence he came nothing new, after all, beneath the ancient moon? The questions occurred to Orcus, but he made no attempt to answer them. He really did not care, one way or the other.)

Not only evil powers had been brought into objective reality by the Change. From earth and sea and sky there welled into existence other forms of inhuman but intelligent life. The Change that had damped the energies of nuclear fire had at the same time freed the energies of life. The nameless force that lay behind both kinds of energy could not, ultimately, be repressed; that which was inherent in every atom could not be destroyed.

Gradually the elemental powers of earth and sea and air came to be looked on as allies by that portion of humanity who chose the West, against the men and women who had elected to associate themselves with demons, and who with the demons had formed that society of essential selfishness called the East. How the name of East and West had come to be used rather than, say, North and South, or Red and Green, was no longer remembered in Rolf's day. Nor would such a question ever have had any significance for Orcus.

Dominating the other quasimaterial powers of the East, and leading them in slowly intensifying war against the West, Orcus the Demon-Patriarch sought slaves and allies among the beasts of the planet as well as among the men. A race of intelligent flying reptiles had evolved in the mere thousands of years that had passed since the Change, so life-rich had the substance of the world become. These reptiles became close allies of the demonic powers, just as a species of huge, intelligent, nocturnal birds, the reptiles' natural enemies, came into being and joined the West.

Still, humanity was at the heart of the struggle. Only humans were capable of dealing with both beasts and spirits on their own terms. People had largely deserted the technology that had enabled

them to Change the world. But before their forget-
fulness could become complete, the pressure of the
new war made them try to recall and rebuild what
they had lost. Thus it was that the technology of the
Old World had never entirely died.

Orcus grasped how vitally important human beings were to the struggle, but when he began to train
and organize his human slave-allies he underestimated their true potential. There was among the
first generation of his recruits a man so consistently
successful in his assigned tasks, and at the same
time so apparently common and predictable in his
motives (therefore as trustworthy as anyone in the
East could be) that Orcus promoted him time and
again. The human did well in each succeeding job,
and accomplished each without giving the appearance of more ambition than a human being (in Orcus' view) should have. Eventually the man was
given command not only of other humans, but of
lesser demons as well. So John Ominor advanced,
using skillfully the centuries of extra life with which
his demon-master was pleased to reward him.

Perhaps Orcus, who had never fully understood
men, never understood himself either. He may have
come gradually to think himself omnipotent, and so
grew careless. Whatever the explanation, without a
hint of warning, he was tricked and overthrown by
the man Ominor. John Ominor, with the men and
demons he had suborned to aid him, cast down the
demon-emperor Orcus and bound him in perpetual
slumber. Orcus was not slain, could not be slain,
because his life could not be found. Nor could he be
made to reveal where it was. It was as if he did not
know. The victorious new lords of the East were
puzzled; the circumstances of Orcus' birth, that
would have explained much, were unknown to
them.

As was the existence of Ardneh.

Still the war against the West went on, as bitter as
ever, and now more slowly, for Orcus' power was

sorely missed by the East. But to awaken him
enough to use him properly would be very dangerous. He was kept bound with certain other un-
trustworthy powers, under the world, in darkness
and tormented sleep. The fitful flashes of con-
sciousness that came amid his dreams he spent
constructing scenarios of revenge.

Riding a griffin-like, demonic steed that galloped
in midair across the demon-haunted night, the
gnarled sorcerer known as Wood flew northwest
among the clouds. He had been Ominor's ac-
complice in the overthrow of Orcus, and he was
Ominor's chief wizard still. He and his mount had
risen from the vast encampment of the army of the
East, and he was flying to seek out the Constable's
small force where it was resting in its frustrated
pursuit of Rolf of the Broken Lands.

Wood's mount flew faster than any beast or man
could travel or ever had, unless it were some Old
World master of the technologies of speed. The tall
clouds of a midsummer storm glowed with muffled
lightning to right and left as Wood flashed between
them. The demon-beast, whose shaggy back he
rested on, ran silently on air. Its griffin's hooked-
beak eagle-head bobbed and swayed at the end of
the long neck, along which feather and scale com-
mingled. Its wings spread and sailed, seemingly no
more than banners or balances as it ran on wind and
nothingness with driving, pounding legs. This steed
would carry no other human not even Ominor himself.

In the flicker of lightning, Wood's face was grim.
Out here in the northern hinterland something was
going very dangerously wrong. When the Constable
had sent his first appeal for magical help of the
highest order it had seemed likely he was trying to
cover up some blunder made by his own wizard, or
by himself. But now in Wood's own auguries the
ominous portents had grown too grave and numer-

ous to ignore. Some of the very highest powers of the West must be fighting hard to foil Abner's efforts in this obscure place.

Now already the demon-griffin's course was slanting down, angling steeply toward the gently rolling land dimly visible below. The prairie came clearer now, where the scudding cloud-shadows let the moonlight fall. Down the griffin flew toward one particular grove on the tree-sprinkled expanse, a grove where torches burned, protecting huddled reptiles against marauding birds. The arrival of Wood and his demon-steed under those trees opened all the reptiles' eyes and made of them glittering beads in the flaring torchlight. With a mixture of wariness and relief Abner's handful of human soldiers watched Wood dismount.

With a single, secret word Wood hobbled his baleful mount. Leaving it standing in the middle of the camp, he strode toward the door of the tent where the Constable's banner hung limply from a staff. Before the magician reached the tent Abner emerged from it, looking weary and on guard, to greet him with the gestures appropriate for welcoming an equal.

Entering the large tent, Wood caught just a glimpse of loveliness, of a golden, impossibly graceful body rising hastily from a couch and vanishing behind a hanging partition of rich silk, trailing unbelievable blond hair. He had to think that the timing was deliberate, that he was meant to see what he had seen.

Wood was not noticeably perturbed. Without further preamble, he demanded of Abner: "What is delaying matters here?"

Abner spread his massive hands. "Western magic. Why else should I call upon you? The so-called magician you have furnished me seems utterly unable to cope with what is being done to us."

His suspicions confirmed, Wood nodded gravely and closed his eyes. He let himself be thoroughly aware of the thin tent-floor just beneath his feet, of the grass pressed down under that, of tree-branches not very far overhead (and of the golden woman somewhere nearby, getting dressed; had she been distracting Abner from business? most men's effectiveness would have been impaired with her around), and of the soldiers and the sleepy reptiles and of his own most savage mount outside. Wood was adapting, submerging himself into the psychic climate of the place, letting its energy patterns inform his mind. At first, nothing seemed much out of the ordinary. But he persisted, and, in a little while, sighed and opened his eyes.

"Ardneh has taken the field against you," he said then to the Constable. "He is exceedingly subtle, and it is little wonder that your wizard has been unaware of what is setting all his work at naught. I could perhaps have been deceived myself had I not met Ardneh the day we summoned him to our capital. I will always know him now."

Abner nodded slowly. "Then what do you advise? Does it make any sense for me to press on with forty men against him?"

"You must press on, with whatever men you have, and gather more as fast as you can bring them here. Our whole future is turning on what is going to happen, somewhere not far from here to the northwest."

"And Ardneh? Can you clear him from my path?"

"I can," Wood said brusquely, "with the powers I shall soon invoke to help me with the job. Within a day or two, if not tonight . . . I mean to make a trial of it tonight."

He made a short gesture of farewell and strode out of the tent. When he had swung himself astride his steed, Wood cast about him by his arts until he was able to sense the location of the two fugitive humans whose capture had so far been beyond the powers of the East. They were resting now, it appeared, not many kilometers distant.

"One of them labors under some kind of minor curse," Wood commented, to the Nameless One, who had appeared from somewhere and was now standing motionless a little distance off. "Your doing, I suppose?"

"I . . . yes, great Lord." The Nameless One bowed as if in modesty.

Wood nodded, not troubling to find out the details. It was remarkable that the man had been able to accomplish even that much against the opposition that he faced here. "Well done. But now restrain yourself to a defensive posture for a time."

"As you will, Lord."

Wood dug heels into the cold flanks of his riding-demon, and into the ear that it unfolded for him, he whispered the needful word. With a roar of sound they rocketed into the air. Once above the treetops, he again turned his mount's massive, sharp-beaked head into the north. This time he was content to fly at low altitude, and he did not urge the griffin to anything like full speed. He meant to test the strength of Ardneh to the full this night, and to destroy it if he could, without undergoing a desperate risk himself. But there was no great hurry about it; he did not expect to be able to take Ardneh by surprise. To Wood, the something-out-of-the-ordinary that was Ardneh was coming clearer now, bit by bit in tantalizing glimpses like the one he had had of Abner's concubine. Subtle hints of splendid powers, and of a beauty that could not, unless it were a lie or under some evil bond, could not be any part of the Empire of the East.

After watching Wood's violent departure, Abner started to mouth an informal curse, thought better of it (Wood would never be so foolish as to try to kick Abner in the shins), and instead walked a quick tour of inspection around the perimeter of his little camp. Satisfied that his sentries were properly alert, his reptiles well guarded by burning torches, and that no other business needed his attention at the moment, he went back to his tent.

She had returned to the couch. Amid disordered draperies she stretched out in a pose half sleepy and half sensual, like some fine catlike beast. Her eyes were nearly closed, but there was a tremor of candlelight along the length of their golden lashes, and Abner knew she was looking at him, as he brought down his palm to snuff the candle out.

Now for a little while the Constable forgot the world outside his tent. Soon, however, there came some sounds of movement at its door, hesitant and tentative sounds, but threatening unwelcome interruption. He could picture the Nameless One there, or some of his officers shifting their feet, listening to ascertain if anything urgent was going on inside. They were bearing news but were uncertain of its importance. They thought the Constable should be told, but were afraid of his anger if they bothered him at the wrong time for something that turned out to be trivial. Would they go away? No, at any moment now they would work up the nerve to stop their exchange of silent gestures with the sentry and call out to be admitted.

He got up and without bothering to dress went to the door, and in displeased tones demanded: "What is it, what do you want?"

The darkness was greater in the tent than just outside, and even as Abner spoke he saw there was no sentry, only a figure taller than the Nameless One or any of his officers, tall as Abner himself. Abner was alerted before his answer came, was already moving back to where his sword hung in its scabbard on the tent's central pole.

"My wife," the tall stranger said, matter-of-factly, and drove in a sword-thrust that no man could have seen coming, much less avoided, in that poor light. But neither could the stranger see Abner well, and the blade did no more than slice tent-cloth and splinter innocent wood.

Abner had his own sword in his hand by now, and his lungs were filling for the bellow that would rouse the camp, when other screams shattered the night outside. "Rally to me!" roared out the Constable, and cut at the dim figure of his adversary, missing as his attacker had.

Now the man was inside the tent, and suddenly the darkness was no longer deep. Some neighboring tent had burst up into flames, almost explosively, and sent a tawny flaring light into the Constable's. The noise outside had mounted up as well, sounds not only of fighting but of panic, and at the moment that augured ill for the Eastern cause. Abner's place was outside, but his way was barred. His second thrust at his foe was parried with impressive speed and strength; the man blocking the doorway was certainly not going to be readily brushed aside. The enemy cut savagely back at Abner's legs, a blow that might have taken one off clean if it had landed; Abner dismissed a half-formed idea of turning and cutting his way out through the tent wall, to reach and lead his men. The first moment he turned his back upon this enemy would be the last he lived.

"Chairmian," Abner called softly, in a moment's lull after the next violent passage of arms. The next words he meant to say were *strike at him from behind*, but before he could utter them, something made him aware of the treacherous blow coming at the rear of his own skull, something hard and heavy swung by thin girlish arms. Abner started to turn and block the blow, realized that the sword would get him if he did, and tried to throw himself on the floor and roll from between his enemies, knowing even as he did so that he was too late. And he wondered, even as the sword came butchering between his ribs, how he had ever thought that the East, whose essence was treachery, could ever stand.

Speeding at treetop level to the north, Wood

dreamed briefly of glory. If he could return to the Emperor with the jewel in his possession and the crushing of Ardneh to his personal credit, certain key members of the Emperor's council might be persuaded that Wood would be a more effective Emperor than Ominor . . .

The taste of that thought was delightful, but it was a sweetness forbidden until the coming battle with Ardneh had been won.

It was an easy matter for Wood to cast his vision ahead to where the two fugitives rested. They were in some kind of cave, and the protection of Ardneh could be sensed around them. Wood could see how to reach them. It turned out, however, that reaching them was another matter. No sooner had he turned his mount directly toward the fugitives than a wind sprang up in his face. The wind quickly rose to a shrieking intensity, and Wood realized at once that its energies were more than strictly physical. It buffeted the griffin-demon and tried to turn him back. Wood dug in his heels. His mount snorted flame and continued to make headway. Then came a gust of superb violence. The demon-steed was halted in his airborne gallop, shot flying upward like a windborne leaf, sent skidding and pawing along a scudding firmament of clouds. The psychic energies that were the stuff of wizardry came forth from Ardneh's stronghold in a torrent to match that of the driving air.

Even under the spur of Wood's threats and incantations, his steed could make no headway, and soon he was forced to let it turn and ride before the blast. Most onlookers would have thought his situation precarious indeed, but Wood was not greatly perturbed. He had expected more subtlety on Ardneh's part than this. The wind was driving him back momentarily, but it should not be too difficult to cope with.

Muttering words that seemed to be torn uncompleted from his lips by the twisting wind, Wood called powers to his aid. From odd places on the earth and under it he called up a motley horde of demon auxiliaries, the strongest force he could assemble in one time and place at a few moments' notice. Ardneh must fall before this group should he dare to try to stand and fight them. If Ardneh would not fight he must retreat, and yield the two he was protecting.

The wind had slowly died as Wood had ceased to challenge it. Now, when his ill-favored troop of demons was fully assembled, grimacing and cackling like gigantic reptiles as they circled Wood on various shapes of wings amid the flying murk, he reined his mount in a wide circle and once more charged into the north.

The shell of demonic forces now surrounding Wood and his mount kept out the wind at first, when Ardneh tried to force them back again. Like some Old World missile the knot of Eastern power that Wood had formed around himself pushed its way through the blast. But the wind now rose to a new height of violence, and black clouds hurtling through it struck like fists upon the demons' shell. And now from Ardneh's striking fists there lanced out bolts of lightning. Like the wind, the lightning was deeply charged with energies beyond the physical range, and each bolt was well aimed. Some flew at the demons surrounding Wood, and some were meant for him. His utmost mental agility was needed to detect the bolts that were to be aimed at him while they were still in the process of formation, and to defuse them, drain their power before they flew, when they would be too fast for any mortal man to stop.

Some of Wood's host of conscripted warriors were fast enough to parry lightning directed at themselves. Nor could they be slain by it, for all their lives were safely hidden elsewhere. But Ardneh's hail of darts came thick and fast upon them now, painful, damaging, red-hot, impossible to stand against.

The demons' shell of force was pierced and broken, and once more Wood's powerful mount was gripped by Ardneh's wind-blast and hurled back. The griffin was flung twenty kilometers downwind before the hurricane abated enough for Wood to once more summon his demonic outriders around him. Whipped and half-stunned they came, mountainously cringing, shrinking their physical volumes as much as they could in order to make less conspicuous targets for his expected wrath. With words of terrible power Wood lashed them forward, northward, once again. This time he himself remained riding his griffin in a slow circle in this area of greater safety; trying to think, trying to probe ahead and understand.

By his arts he saw his demons driving north, beyond the clouds of driving mist that lay between. To meet them now came Ardneh's lightning, this time a single swordblade, flickering, walking along the energy spectrum through all the bands where demons had their half-material existence.

Yet again Wood's troops were thrown back, in fear and agony; and now at last they had found the enemy more terrible than Wood, and however he cursed and threatened they would not go into the north again. He sharpened his incantations yet more, wreaked suffering upon his quivering vassals, and banished them to hidden dungeons till they should be useful once again. Now, however, he was calm in all his curses and punishings. He no longer raged. He saw now that a little more effort from his demons would not have helped; they were simply not strong enough to stand against Ardneh.

How could Wood have so grievously underestimated his enemy's strength? Had Ardneh somehow managed a tremendous accession of power recently?

It was not simply that Ardneh was powerful enough to defeat them. Most shattering was the realization that the devastating defense had not even occupied Ardneh's full attention. While watching the last defeat of his demon-troop, Wood for the first time had managed—or had been permitted—to perceive the extent of Ardneh's world-wide activities. It was a frightening disclosure. Ardneh could not have possessed such strength for long, Wood realized, or the East would have lost the war some time ago instead of now thinking itself on the verge of victory.

In the form Wood's vision took, Ardneh appeared in the guise of a tall, powerful man, striding through a pack of curs that swirled snapping and growling vainly around his legs. The dog named Wood received no more attention and effort than was necessary in order to beat him off; meanwhile Ardneh's chief attention was directed somewhere else, somewhere Wood's dream-perception could not follow.

Lies, Wood told himself, and felt somewhat relieved; lies. Propaganda, put into his mind to intimidate and weaken him. But he had no evidence that it was lies. And if such a trick could be worked on him, and he could not tell it was a trick, he might well be facing an enemy who could destroy him.

—*in the nick of time he realized that Ardneh was coming at him for the kill*—

His host had been dispersed. He turned and fled, the lightning-bolts pursuing him downwind. Wood lived through it, although his demon-steed was struck so violently it lost the power of flight. All of Wood's arts that remained useful to him now barely availed to save his life, to let him tumble from his falling mount into rain-sodden bushes, amid a scene of wild storm and waving branches. Bruised and shaken and winded, but not seriously hurt, he realized that Ardneh had departed, and that he

himself was within a kilometer or two of the camp
where he had left the Constable.

Limping and cursing his way through the marshy
grass and rain, Wood knew that the ultimate powers
available to the East would have to be invoked.

VIII

They Open Doors,
They Take Down Bars

———◆—◆—◆———

Wood, stumbling on scratched and weary legs toward the Constable's camp, rehearsing in his mind what he might say to make his arrival there appear less inglorious, was within a hundred meters of his goal when he heard the surprise attack led by Chup burst out ahead of him.

After the first shock, Wood was not really surprised. The night belonged to the West, and it was not the first time an Eastern position thought secure had been taken unawares. He paused, trying to determine what was going on ahead. The enemy force seemed quite small. Ardneh was nowhere near. Wood had no functional demons to call on at the moment, but still, after his moment's assessment of the situation, he pressed on at a hurried walk. His personal anger was aroused, instead of the rest and food and drink he had been looking forward to, here was only another fight. But his rage was cold and eager. The smart of his defeat by Ardneh would be eased by victory here; instead of appearing humbled before the Constable, he would come in as a savior. There were fires ahead, and screams of panic. The East was not doing very well at the moment.

It was for good reason that Wood was accounted the greatest wizard of the East. When swords were out and blood was spilled, it was difficult for any magician to raise an effective spell—the Nameless

One even now lay bleeding out his life ahead, Wood's extra senses told him—but Wood's arts were still powerful, even now when his best powers had been scattered and his most potent energies exhausted. He still had one vital advantage, that of surprise, fully as important for the magician as for the soldier. . . .

On legs that no longer felt tired and injured, Wood approached the camp, where shadowy figures ran and fought before the burning tents. It took him a moment to make sure that there was no Western wizard among the attackers who might be capable of serious opposition to Wood's spells. The fat one who had earlier, with Ardneh's help, overcome the efforts of the Nameless One was there, but that meant nothing to Wood, as Ardneh himself was still absent from the scene.

Standing in the shadows of a tree near the edge of the burning camp, a vantage point from which he could see without readily being seen, Wood pronounced one lengthy word and began to make small gestures with one hand. The fat Western wizard was the first to fall, whirling round almost gracefully, elaborate talismans spilling from his hands like so much trash, before he tumbled like a chopped-through tree. One after another, as they came into Wood's view, the other men of the Western raiding party fell, backs arching, twisting in convulsions. There seemed to be less than a dozen of them in all, even fewer than Wood had thought at first. They could do nothing against Wood because he gave them no time to find him with their blades. One of their leaders came closest. A tall man, he emerged from the Constable's tent with bloodied sword held high. Seeing Wood, or somehow sensing his position, the Westerner charged like a maddened beast. But though his long strides brought him so close that Wood had to dodge back at the last moment from the killing blade, it was the Westerner who fell.

He was the last, except for one or two who might

have managed to run away; in his depleted and exhausted state Wood did not care to make the effort to be sure of that. All the others lay on the earth, their convulsions quieting as Wood led them smoothly into ensorceled slumber. Those he had felled were still alive, and he had a good reason for keeping them so.

The surviving Eastern soldiers who had survived were gathering in the center of the camp once more. Wood called to a junior officer and charged him with seeing to it that the prisoners were gathered together and kept alive until they should be needed. But no sooner had Wood finished giving these orders than he looked up to see that the golden girl he had earlier glimpsed in Abner's tent had emerged from some hiding place or other clad now in a silken robe, and was raising a dagger over one of the prone Westerners.

"Forebear, girl!" Wood called out. "We have far weightier business than your grievance against this wretch, whatever it may be. Where is the Constable?"

The golden woman threw down her dagger and turned to Wood. Now she was the picture of submission. "Alas, my lord Wood, the Constable is dead. At the last minute, when the enemy had already entered the camp, he saw the danger and met it bravely. He did what he could, but it was not enough."

Wood nodded, unsurprised, then looked around and raised his voice. "Where is the senior surviving officer, then?"

When that man had made himself known, Wood questioned him: "Have you enough able troops to defend this site until the dawn? There can hardly be a dozen live Westerners within ten kilometers of us at the moment. I will be available to help in an emergency, but not for keeping watch. There is another task upon which I must concentrate. I want to know if I can safely relax my vigilance to do so."

"Aye, aye, my Lord, I think so. We have at least twenty men still on their feet. These Westerners can move soft as demons. Our sentries had their throats cut—"

"That should keep their successors awake, at least for a few hours. Now I am going to set to work, and you must detail two men to fetch and carry for me. That you may cooperate intelligently with me, I will give you some explanation." He paused; the woman was watching him, round-eyed, and some of the soldiers were gawking dazedly. Wood took the officer by the arm and led him to one side; and he made his own image change in the eyes of the gawkers, to something that was not fit to look upon, and they hastened about their business. Then to the officer Wood said: "I have tonight met Ardneh face to face, and have found his strength grown awesome. I can only guess at how he has managed to augment his powers; now they are enough to tip the scales of the entire war against the East."

The officer was sweating, evidently wishing he was a private simply taking orders once again. Wood went on: "It will be necessary to call up some special reserves. I am referring to a group of demons who have for one reason or another been put into confinement, in a place—outside the normal world. They are dangerous and unruly creatures, and I must impress upon you the necessity of my being allowed to concentrate in peace while I am working with them."

All that Wood had said thus far was true. His great untruth had been in leaving out even the faintest hint of the existence of Orcus, the real object of the work he was about to do. Not even in his own inner thoughts had Wood allowed himself to form that name. Not for centuries now.

The officer wet his lips. "Great Lord, you will understand that I mean you no disrespect, when I venture the opinion that this project of releasing imprisoned demons, along with these discoveries regarding our enemy Ardneh, should be reported to headquarters as soon as possible. To the Emperor himself."

The officer was sharper and bolder than he looked. Understanding that the man wanted to be reassured that there was no intrigue against the Emperor in progress here—or perhaps wanted to be let in on it if there were—Wood answered patiently. "Send a message to headquarters any time you like. But I presume no reptile will fly until daylight, and I must begin the evocation here and now. Tonight. It is not a calling that can be made in an hour, or even in a day. There are many bars to be let down, sealed doors to be broken, locks to be opened for which the keys were thrown away. If we are to have help against Ardneh in time, I must begin now to call upon—the powers that are to help us. Should the Emperor for some unimaginable reason forbid me to go through with the calling, I can stop it at any point. Now if you will detail the men to help me, I must select the first required victim."

The officer was reassured, and moved away, giving his men such orders as Wood had requested.

When Wood came to the Western prisoners, he found them now laid out in a row, all still unconscious from the effects of his paralyzing spells. The woman was standing there, once more looking down at one of the still forms. The same one. It was he who had come near killing Wood. This time her expression indicated thought, rather than uncaring hate.

It was Wood's first opportunity for a long, close look at her. "What is your name, girl?"

"I am called Charmian, my noble Lord." Her blue eyes were so luminous that his spell-casting fingers twitched defensively. But it was no more than woman's inborn witchery she had, as power to bedazzle men. No *more*? There were numerous demonic spells not half so powerful. Wood pondered the possible advantages and drawbacks of sending her on as a gift to Ominor; the Emperor enjoyed alluring women as much as any ordinary man.

Wood looked down. "And who is this one at your feet, who makes you frown so thoughtfully?"

"He was my husband, Lord," she said, managing to surprise him. She hesitated briefly before adding: "There is a question I would ask." His expression gave assent, and she went on: "You are choosing one of these for a ritual victim? I thought as much . . . is the victim's death to be an easy one or difficult?"

"Tonight's victim will die easily."

"Then I beg of you, dread Lord, take some other than this who was my bridegroom once. I would not have him die a quick and easy death."

Duncan's camp tonight was nearer to Ardneh, by some kilometers, than it had been the night before. Duncan each day moved his army north, following his wizards' advice and his own intuition, and keeping pace with the parallel movement of the main body of his Eastern foes.

Now in Duncan's tent, the seeress Anita, in deep trance, was muttering: " . . . they open doors to they know not what, they take down bars that were put up when they were wiser and more frightened." The girl's speech began to trail off, becoming more disjointed and unintelligible, until at last she could only cry out in unwonted fear. Duncan, weary from the dull riding and intermittent fighting of the day, tried to puzzle out what it could mean, but he could not. Neither could his wizards, who contradicted one another in sharp debate about the girl: whether to waken her or send her deeper into trance, whether what she said tonight had any useful meaning. At last she was taken out. Duncan and his councilors continued meeting through the night. There was no communication from Ardneh.

The blood of the first sacrifice was warm and fresh on Wood's hands, and in his throat the words

of power flowed like song, controlled, in harmony
with the images formed in his mind by his practiced
imagination. Energy flowed through him, from him.
Shortly after starting the evocation he had felt a
pang of worry, on realizing just how tired he was.
This was not a task to be begun when weary; mis-
takes might be punished terribly. But now it was all
going well enough.

It was a task that required a full mastery of magic,
but he was equal to it. More than equal. In his imagination he was now descending worn stone steps,
through a dark and narrow passage, going to visit
the dungeon under the world. Other demons were
confined there as well as Orcus, and Wood meant to
release them in passing. They were not really
dangerous—not to Wood. Now he could hear them,
feel them, smell them, moving in some imagined cell
just off his passageway. A pack of ethereal wolves,
jostling one another for the chance at taking on
reality once more. They knew their jailer was coming, and perhaps they knew he meant to let them
out.

To Wood these were not much; they were cattle he
penned up or loosed, no matter how monstrous and
powerful they might loom in the sight of lesser men.
To handle them he needed no protracted cere-
monies, no human sacrifices; he could bring them
up into the world tonight, without consulting the
Emperor, and he meant to do so. It was only the
Other, whose name Wood had been avoiding even in
his thoughts, that made him worry now. It was the
process of releasing Orcus, of course keeping hold
enough on him to put him down again when the
West had been defeated, that called for supreme
wizardry and offerings of lives.

Now the first victim had been offered, and down
in the deepest dungeon cell the chained One had
begun to stir and tremble in his painful sleep. When
those stirrings became evident to Wood, their mag-
nitude restored his memory regarding what Orcus

was truly like. Suddenly he now longer saw the gathering of the other outcast demons as a wolf-pack, even as a herd of unruly cattle, but as no more than a nest of squealing, snapping rats. Neither they or Wood had changed of course. It was only the comparison with Orcus.

Wood slowed his imagined descent of the stone steps. The bottom was near. Surprisingly, Orcus was not only stirring, not only beginning to awaken, he was already straining and struggling to be free. He radiated an incredible power and purpose. Impossible, of course, that his effort should succeed. Wood was still the jailer, armed and comfortable and with the stair behind him open for his ascent. He stood now at the ultimate cell door, looking down through bars and gratings at the wretch in chains, the giant cramped and bound. But the rousing of Orcus had begun too successfully, was proceeding a little too rapidly. To maintain the proper margin of safety, steps should be taken to slow things down.

The bloodied ritual knife still in his hand, the corpse of the first sacrifice still warm at his feet, Wood swayed a little with his weariness, swayed and frowned and changed the text that he was chanting, altered the shape of the dungeon whose symbol-structure was held so carefully in his mind . . .

Like a snake uncoiling from the uttermost depths beneath the world, the power Orcus came striking up at him. Through symbols and matter alike the shockwave traveled, launched by the half-conscious Demon-Lord, trying in blind fury to strike back at his tormentors. At the first impact of the shockwave, Wood cried out. He had a moment in which to realize that in his weariness he had mispronounced a word of his long chant, before he fell down senseless.

Even with Wood unconscious, the One who had struck him still could not escape his dungeon. The walls and bonds of magic were still too many and too strong. Orcus could not force his way back into the world of men, or even awaken fully from his sleep. But the hords of lesser demons that Wood had been about to herd back into the world were now able to force the passage for themselves. They lost no time in doing so.

Charmian crouched motionless as the vile rabble of the demons began to appear in the torchlit night before her. One after another their hulking, obscure shapes blurred into the world, and almost at once vanished again for other parts of it. Wood when he awoke, or some other magician of comparable stature, could round them up again, and no doubt would; but they were not going to stand still and wait for it.

Charmian had good reason to be afraid. That she herself was of the East might mean very little to these ill-disciplined powers. Any one of them, hungry to inflict pain, or yearning for the taste of some immaterial human essence, might destroy her on impulse—or, worse, swallow her without destroying. Imagine the emotions of a spoiled infant, combined with the force of some huge animal or elemental power, and cleverness above the human average.

To try to run away might draw attention to herself, but still she was on the brink of doing so. She was distracted by the realization that the Western prisoners still alive were now awakening. The light spells Wood had placed on them were loosened by his unconsciousness. No one had thought to bind them physically, or perhaps the thought had been that to do so might insult the chief wizard of the East.

Now Charmian saw her husband stir. An instant later Chup got to his feet. He was only a few meters away, and when his eyes fastened on her she did not dare to run.

He was a more immediate threat than any of the demons, who so far had ignored her as they came into sight and vanished again. She took a step nearer to him, and with hands clasped beseechingly cried out: "Help me, Chup! I've released you, saved your life. You must get me away from here!"

Chup continued looking at her. She read cold rage into his fixed stare, and then realized that it was only blank. Now his forehead wrinkled. With men screaming and demons flickering in the background, he gave the impression of a man with all the time in the world, trying to understand some interesting problem. Now she noted that the other surviving Westerners were wandering around witlessly; their minds must be still half-imprisoned by Wood's spells.

Now she drew back from Chup again, but he moved with her, studying her face as if he sought some answer there. She feared to turn and run lest some predator's instinct make him chase her and attack. "Come, Chup! I beg of you. Save me! Help me get away!" The Constable was dead, Wood fallen, and demons seemed to rule the world. There was nowhere else for Charmian to turn. She pleaded, tugged at Chup's unyielding arm, and at last in her desperation slapped his face. This last made him frown at her most villainously, though he gave no sign of retaliation. The frown frightened Charmian, and she hastened to soothe him with strokings and soft words. His face smoothed and he looked content once again, while above him and Charmian the insubstantial horrors of demons came and went, casting light of purple and gold and green, and leaving waves of sickness in the air.

An Eastern soldier, probably maddened by some passing demon's touch, came bounding at them. Chairmian saw his contorted face and his uplifted sword. She turned to try to run, but slipped and fell. As the man leaped toward her, Chup caught him by one arm, seemed to wave him in midair as if he were a banner, and threw him sprawling on his face, so heavily that he did not rise.

Recovering, Charmian crawled to pick up the sword the man had dropped. Murmuring "Come, My Lord Chup, come with me. We will help each other," she held it out toward Chup, whose hand closed on the pommel as naturally as a mouth might close on food. Taking hold of his other hand, big and hard, docile and trusting, Charmian led him out away from the remains of smoldering tents and torches, away from the passing pyrotechnic demons, out into the summer night. Other humans could be heard running and crying out around them in the dark, but no one paid them any heed.

IX

Ardneh's Life

———◆———

"Wolf tracks, if I've ever seen them" Rolf announced. It was mid-morning on the day after their arrival at Ardneh's base. They had camped overnight wrapped in their cloaks in a small, ancient dormitory, where the plumbing still worked but the ancient furnishings had otherwise crumbled long ago. Ardneh, still busy integrating into his own complex being the strange artifact that had been their gift, had not yet explained to them in any detail what their chief tasks here were to be. But he had asked them to make a short reconnaissance round the old mine entrance, to see if there were any signs of their having been followed. When this request puzzled them, Ardneh explained: "It is here, inside my own physical structure, that my powers are in some ways most limited." And there came to Rolf, with seeming naturalness, the mental image of a hand trying to bandage itself.

Now he stood with Catherine at the mouth of the ancient adit. A thunderstorm had come and gone during the night, unheard by them inside, leaving fresh mud where the small stream's banks had been dry dirt. The splayed prints in the mud were those of large and heavy animals. "Only natural beasts of some kind, we can hope," Rolf added now.

"Look." Catherine was pointing at the hard rock ledge a couple of meters in from the entrance. Rolf crouched beside her. The faint smear of mud on rock was not yet quite dry. His eyes could not really make it into a large paw-print. But something, or someone, had left it there within the last few hours.

"Are there wolves that serve the East?" Catherine asked.

"I have heard stories of such, but never seen them. Ardneh will know."

"We were to scout outside; I suppose we had better not retreat at the mere sight of a track."

Rolf agreed, and they proceeded cautiously. But, once away from the mud at the adit's entrance, they could discover no evidence of enemies or large beasts. New rivulets, still gurgling with rainwater, entered the stream at several points, and a hundred meters downstream from Ardneh's cave it was now much deeper than it had been, overtopping its normal banks to comb long grass with its current.

After following the stream that far they scouted in a circle centered on the entrance to the cave. They climbed the hill, crawling cautiously round its grassy top to observe a peaceful summer world in all directions. From there the circle brought them back to the stream and its swift pools. Catherine knelt to scan the bank closely; her thighs showed white before her skirt fell back demurely into place.

The little glade felt utterly secure, isolated from friend and foe alike. A thought that Rolf had banished came leaping back, with power irresistible: *Maybe the curse has ended now —*

Two minutes later, feeling numb with fury, he was turning away from Catherine, picking up his just-dropped scabbard from the grass. The sword came out into his right hand, and with it he hacked murderously at the Lady Charmian's image, projected by his rage on a small tree. He was leaving marks to show enemy scouts that someone had been here. All right, then, he was leaving marks.

"I am changed again," came Catherine's wearily steady voice from behind him. "Changed and dressed."

Walking behind her, on their silent way back to

the cave, he thought that even her normal, youthful
shape was after all far from lovely. Those bare legs
moving ahead of him were not curved in the way
that a man's dreams told him a girl's legs should be
curved. Too thin and wiry. My Lady Charmian
chooses ugly servants, always—

And Rolf felt sullen, mean, and ugly too.

Wood woke with a start, and instantly sprang to
his feet. The movement came in a burst of fear-born
energy that drained away as quickly as it had come,
and left him tottering. He stood swaying in the
cheerful sunlight, amid unfamiliar grass and trees,
unable to recall how he had come to be here.

Gradually, in bits and pieces, it came back: the
error made in weariness, the jolting punishment
from Orcus. But that had been during the night, and
it was late morning now. Or might it even be early
afternoon—

With a shock Wood beheld that the grass where he
had lain still remained pressed down, showing the
outline of his body. Within the outline it was even
yellowed, beginning to die from lack of sun.

How many days had he been lying there? Within
the outline of withered grass, beetles were scurrying
to find new shade. But though he must have been
motionless as a corpse, apparently no living thing
had come closer than that to molesting him. A magician of Wood's power was not completely unpro-
tected even when unconscious.

Now he looked cautiously about. The only other
humans remaining in the grove had made food for
scavengers already. He faced no immediate threat.

Wood spewed out words of power, barking com-
mands and questions into the air, which soon
crackled with invisible presences. His first orders
were for food and drink—he was ravenous and
thirsty now, as well as stiff in every muscle and joint.
Next he demanded information.

What he learned was, for the most part, reassur-

ing. The horde of rogue demons had scattered
around the world, which was an annoyance, but no
more—obviously Orcus had not escaped. Quickly
Wood set in motion the processes necessary to
bring the others back under his control. Then,
clumsy and aching, he set out on foot across tree-
dotted grassland in the direction where, as his invisible informants now assured him, Ominor's army
was presently encamped.

With no better means of travel than his old legs,
the journey was slow. But the kind of steed he had
once ridden was not readily replaceable, and he was
saving his powers now for essentials. After an hour,
however, the hiking grew oppressively difficult. He
took thought, noted that the light breeze was at his
back, and nodded to himself with satisfaction. With
a few words he changed his shape into that of a
wind-rolled, rootless weed, a feat he could manage
with no great expenditure of energy.

In this guise he traveled faster than before, and by
late afternoon had come within sight of his goal.
Resuming his usual shape, he now made himself
completely invisible, a condition hard to maintain
for more than a brief time. In this way he passed
sentries and minor wizards alike without being detected, until he stood inside the pavilion of the Emperor himself. Wood was surprised—though not
enormously so—to discover the woman Charmian
standing before Ominor. She was simply dressed
now, and shy-looking, with downcast eyes. There
were a few other people about.

The dialogue between the Emperor and Charmian was interesting to Wood, as it somewhat concerned him; but the first time John Ominor's eyes
flicked his way they seemed for just a moment to
rest directly on Wood, and after that Wood could no
longer completely convince himself that his invisibility was proof against the Emperor's gaze. A fear
that he could not master began to grow in Wood,
and with a faint shudder he retreated, passing out

through the pavilion walls as a demon might, or
smoke; and once outside he looked for a suitable
place nearby where he might let himself be seeable
again.

To Charmian, John Ominor was saying, in his cus-
tomary loud, half-angry tone: "You still seem surprised at the sight of me, girl. What did you think I
would be like?"

"That you would be impressive, Lord. As indeed
you are."

The Emperor half smiled, and enjoyed looking at
Charmian a little longer before answering her. "As
indeed I am not, you mean. Not loathesome or
demonic-looking. Or even particularly handsome."
Though as usual the Emperor gave the impression
of impatience, yet he was in no hurry to conclude
the conversation. "I have heard of you, most memor-
able lady," he went on. "Attempted to attach yourself to Som the Dead, in the Black Mountains; yes,
and nearly thawed him back to life, didn't you? I can
well believe it . . . though that man always seemed
quite inhuman to me. Whereas I am an ordinary
man in all but power. The powers I was born with,
and those I have since accumulated—rather greater
than those of Som. Or anyone else. Charmian, you
will find my desires much more ordinary than those
of many other men whom you have tried to please;
that is not to say that I am easily satisfied."

"My Emperor, I wish only that I may someday be
granted the privilege of trying to satisfy your
every—"

"To take whatever I want. To punish all my overt
enemies, and to maintain fear in all who are too
frightened of me to be my enemies at the moment—what more is the East but this?"

Charmian, in silence, made deep obeisance toward the carved chair in which the Emperor sat.

Ominor said: "Before you attempt more energetic
ways of contributing to my happiness, answer me a

question or two; repeat to me how you and the man
came to be out there where you were found by my
patrol. What went wrong with Abner, and what has
become of my chief wizard?" There came a hoarse
scream from somewhere not far away, probably
from another chamber of the elaborate tent. "They
are still asking the same questions of the man who
was with you, but it seems he is as witless as he
looked. He does nothing but yelp. You may be our
only witness, so try to remember things in a little
more detail. Exactly where is Wood?"

"My dread Lord, I will do the best I can." Charmian had already told of Abner's fate and Wood's,
leaving out of course her attack on the Constable
from behind. She began to repeat the story now,
adding such detail as she could remember; still she
could not say exactly where it had all happened. She
had wandered for two days with the dazed Chup
before the Eastern patrol found them. She had no
more information about Wood to give the Emperor,
who was listening carefully.

Now and then another mindless outcry drifted in
from Chup. In a moment of private thought it occurred to Charmian how enjoyable it would be to
watch Chup's slow destruction, but then in the next
moment she realized that she would miss him when
he was no more. She recalled feeling a certain joy
mixed with her fear on recognizing him as the man
forcing his way into her rooms at the caravanserai,
and again in the Constable's tent. Of course Chup
might have killed her either time if she had crossed
him; but this man here, on whose favor she was
counting, might well kill her someday for amusement.

John Ominor asked her: "When this group of
demons, as you put it, came pouring out into
the world, was there any one among them
notably larger or more impressive than the rest?"
He seemed to think the question very important.

"I think not, dread Lord, if you can accept the opinion of one not well acquainted with demons, or able to view them without fear."

"No, of course not," Ominor mused, as if to himself, "we would have known." His eye fixed Charmian once more. "And the man with you? He is of the West, you say, and yet you seem to have known him previously?"

There was no telling how much the Emperor might already know, and Charmian now boldly gave the truth. "He was once of the East, my Lord, and he was once my husband. A deserter and a turncoat. I cannot believe his present madness is a sham; but be that as it may, I would be pleased to see his suffering as well as hear it."

Ominor grunted and flicked a glance back over his shoulder. Apparently the signal was relayed and heeded for presently the dismal outcries ceased. A moment more, and two black-garbed torturers came in bringing with them Chup, bound to an iron frame on wheels. He was stripped and bleeding here and there, where patches of skin were missing; but he was not the mangled object Charmian had imagined. His head turned to and fro, eyes glaring wildly.

Another pair of men had come in, wizards to judge by their dress. Ominor now turned to them. "Try some gentler means of restoring his memory. It could be important. If he knows aught of what was befallen Wood—"

There came a hail from outside the pavilion. A stir at the entrance, and then Wood himself appeared there. He hurried forward, scarcely glancing at Charmian, made obeisance, and quickly rose. "A word with you, at once, my Lord."

Ominor arose promptly and led the way out of the chamber, motioning Wood to come along. Charmian was left to contemplate her husband, now being treated kindly, with a mixture of anger and relief that she did not fully understand.

Ominor and Wood confronted one another within
an inner chamber of black silk, a tent within a tent,
guarded round by most dependable powers of se-
crecy, and filled with a darkness that sometimes
could press upon the eye like glaring light.

Wood got to business at once. "Supreme Lord, I
can rouse that man that they are working on out
there; it is one of my spells that still oppresses him.
Has he any information of importance?"

"Not since you are here. Where were you?"

"Mobilizing reserve forces, my lord Emperor. We
shall soon have urgent need of them."

"And you were struck down in the process? So the
woman told me, but I doubted . . . what, who, were
you trying to call up?"

There was a pause. Wood began to answer indi-
rectly. "My Lord, shortly before that I faced Ardneh,
and I was weakened thereby. Ardneh is now might-
ier than we have ever suspected he might become.
He may be as strong as — one other, whom we both
know of, whose name I have not mentioned—"

Ominor stood up. "Are you really leading where I
think you are? Was that the purpose of the ceremony you had begun?" The secret tent muted
sound, but still the anger in his voice was terrible.
"Of course; who else could have struck you down
like that?"

"Lord Emperor, hear me out, if you would save the
East! I tell you I have faced Ardneh and I know! We
must arouse the One whose name should not be
said, to fight for us. Or else we perish."

"*Arouse* him, you say? Not simply tap his power?"

"Yes." Wood swallowed. "Awaken him enough to
send him into battle. Keep reins upon his senses
and his will, and send him back below when he has
served."

There was again a little silence before Ominor
said: "You think it will be possible to release the one
you speak of, then bottle him again like so much
wine?"

"It is a risk that must be taken, supreme Lord."

"You really believe you can do that?" The Emperor's loud crude voice made it sound as if Wood's sanity rather than his ability, was in question.

"Lord, Ardneh had exhausted me before the Other struck me down. Nor could he even then escape our bondage, as you see. Before beginning again I will rest myself, and make thorough preparation. Next time I will have help—"

"Of course!" Ominor clapped his hands, as if blessed with a sudden happy thought. "To help you we must call upon those same three powers that hovered above the lake, and warded harm from our imperial person, the day that we invited Ardneh to our palace—ah, it seems so long ago. Yes, call them, let them clamp shut their jaws upon all who threaten us, as you swore they were eager to do."

Wood hung his head, taking care to indicate nothing but total submission. Ardneh had already driven those three demons from the field, in the cur-pack with the others, as Ominor must understand. Just now was not the time for Wood to say anything more at all.

Having made his point and inspired what he thought to be sufficient fear, the Emperor was ready to talk business. "Wood, despite the recent record of your failures, I find myself listening to this new plan of yours. But I am not yet convinced. I know, better than you or anyone else, the dangers of what you propose. Do not take another step along that road unless I bid you do so. However." Wood's eyes lifted. "However, if what you tell me of Ardneh is true, we may have to take the most desperate steps, and quickly. So rest now, and prepare yourself—are there any preliminary steps remaining?"

Wood was eager once again. "One more sacrifice, great Lord. I need not promise it will be far more carefully conducted than the last. That is all, and the One we speak of will be reachable for quick summoning, or for quickly being reburied as deep as ever.''

There was a silent pause. "Go and do it," said Ominor then abruptly. He stood up, ripped open with his hand the little tent of blackness, and strode out.

Returning to his private quarters, the Emperor was soon visited by one of his chiefs of technology, and by his Master of the Beasts, who came in lupine form. For once, both brought good news. In recent days the technologists' Old World devices had detected a steady increase in electromagnetic activity in a certain small area to the north. It seemed to be precisely where the Beast Master's half-intelligent scouts now reported the scent of two humans, male and female, entering a strange cave. From the same direction had come the winds that had defeated Wood and scattered his demonic horde. In that direction, also, was Duncan's army tending, as if something were there that the Prince wanted to defend.

I have found Ardneh's life. Ominor did not say the words aloud. But he dismissed his aides and stood alone for some time, looking at the map. Then he summoned his field commanders and demanded from them a faster movement to the north. Such beasts as were already near the objective were to try what could be accomplished by a prompt attack.

X

Beast-War

———◆———

"Ardneh, how long will we be here?" Rolf sat on a chest of Old World tools. His hands were playing nervously with a gripping, twisting device of silvery metal. Catherine, on the other side of the room, lay curled up on the floor as if she hoped to sleep. Not many words had passed between the two of them since their return from the scouting expedition. On hearing their report of paw-prints, Ardneh had urged that at least one of them remain awake and alert at all times; they could not depend upon his being able to warn them of danger, here in his own blind interior.

Ardneh's answer to his question now took Rolf by surprise. "The number of days is not now determinable. But almost certainly it will not be as long as a month. By then the outcome of the war will have been decided."

Across the room, Catherine's head came up, her face turned in Rolf's direction.

Rolf opened his mouth, closed it, tried again. "It will be over?" was all that he could find to say at last.

"The next major battle will decide the war," Ardneh replied matter-of-factly. "And it will be fought here, within the month, though the war will not end entirely for another year or two."

"Ardneh . . . fought here?"

"Around me and over me. I must bring the strongest of the enemy to me, and break them here, if they are to be broken at all. And Duncan must come with his army, to be ready to strike again when I have done my utmost."

Catherine asked: "And what are Rolf and I to do?"

"There will be much. Physical repairs and rear-rangements to be made, things I cannot do for my-self, enough work to keep two humans busy until the issue is decided. Rolf has great natural skill in technology; also he is familiar enough with me not to be greatly awed by my presence. Therefore I de-cided that he should be the one to bring me the heart of the power lamp."

Catherine put out a slender hand, to touch a giant piece of hardware. "I have no great skill with things like these."

"More than you know," Ardneh's voice assured her. "You will be of help with the machinery. But your chief value to my plan, the reason I brought you here, lies elsewhere, in the future. I see it dimly, but cannot explain. You have powers that you know not of. Powers of life, that build the world."

"Magic? No, I cannot . . ."

"Not magic. Not un-magic, either. All. Reality."

Her eyes turned to Rolf, as if beseeching him for help. It was a moment of openness between them, such as they had not shared since rejoining Ardneh. But though Rolf's heart went out to that look, he had no other help to give.

Ardneh gave them no time to brood any more, but announced that the integration of the power source that they had brought was now complete. He led them now to other rooms and began to show them some of the tasks they must accomplish. There were interlocking nests of metal and glass to be opened, disassembled, moved, put together again in new configurations. There were long cables, like multi-headed snakes, to be unpacked, tested, and in-stalled. The outward shapes of the machinery were not very complex, but still some practice time was necessary. Rolf's fingers soon got the feel of what was wanted; Catherine, less in tune with technical matters, increasingly limited her help to unpacking, fetching, and carrying, taking up tools only when necessary.

That night in the ruined dormitory, sleep would not come to Rolf. He tossed about for a while, looking again and again at the motionless, cloak-covered form on the far side of the room. Finally he sat up. "Ardneh."

It seemed a long time before an answer came. "What is it?"

"Catherine is under a spell of the Lady Charmian's." The figure on the far side of the room was still apparently asleep. "If you could counteract it, both of us would be grateful."

This time the pause was longer still. Then the voice above Rolf said: "I am aware of the spell. To counteract it would be difficult, because of the source of power that was tapped to make it. And to counteract it does not seem essential."

"Our lives here would be much easier if—"

Calm, inflexible, Ardneh's voice overrode his. "At this moment many lives in the West are more difficult than yours. And there are greater dangers to you than this discomfort that you speak of. I am too busy to even discuss the matter now. Another may help you where I cannot."

Another? Who? But there would be no use in trying to ask; Rolf could feel that Ardneh's presence had departed. Despite himself, despite his awareness of the legless, armless, dying who were far worse off, he half-willingly nursed a sullen anger.

Catherine was still asleep—or still wanted him to think she was. He tried once more to get to sleep himself, but it was hopeless. Getting up, he groped his way through dark but now partially familiar corridors, to the chill cave air of the tunnel and at last to the warmth of summer night outside. For a time he stood cautiously just inside the tunnel mouth, his ears sorting out the natural activities of the prairie night as he heard them through the murmur of the

stream. Then he climbed the little hill above the
entrance to the cave, and sat in the grass to contemplate the stars.

"Whooo, Roolf."

The great bird was almost within reach of his
hand before his eyes could find it in the night.
"Strijeef! It's good to see you again. How are you?
What news?"

The bird spoke briefly of reptiles recently slain,
and personal perils avoided; and then of the march
of great armies, how both East and West were converging on this northern land. "Each day the great
battle that is to come grows nearer. All in Duncan's
army speak of it."

"So says Ardneh, also. Have you a message for me
from Duncan?"

From his courier's pouch Strijeef's nimble talons
brought out a small roll of paper, which he tossed to
Rolf with a flirt of his murderous beak. "Yoouuu are
promoted to captain, and the woman Catherine is
formally enrolled as warrant officer. And there is
one more bit of news, that I bring of my oown sight.
Large four-legged beasts are coming here, loong before either army. A pack of beasts I doo not know,
and they will be here before daylight."

It had rained during the night, and in the dismal
morning the west prairie smelled more of autumn
than of summer. The army of the East was striking
camp, preparing for another day of northward
march. From the earliest light Charmian had been
outside her tent, keeping an alert eye on the tent
where Wood had rested. And now at last she saw
him emerge from it, wearing a soft, rich robe.

Once more a circular space, set apart from other
camp activities, had been made ready for the chief
wizard's intended work. In the middle of that space
Chup had been left waiting through the night, still
bound to his iron frame, and guarded by two soldiers.

Wood had paused, just outside his tent, in conference with other wizards. Charmian took the opportunity to approach the waiting victim. Grabbing
Chup's long hair, she turned his face around to
hers. He snarled, but there was no recognition in the
scarcely-human sound. His eyes were those of a
trapped beast.

Once she had yearned to tear those eyes out with
her nails. Now she had the chance to do so. But
somehow the desire had fled.

Wood was approaching now, followed by two assistants, as silent and somber as their master. At a
flicker of the chief wizard's eyes toward her, Charmian darted out of the circle. Just past its edge, she
paused, alone and watching as before.

As soon as a few preliminaries were out of the
way, Wood came closer to the victim on his iron
frame. The wizard raised and spread his empty
hands. For this sacrifice he must use nothing so
direct as a knife. Subtle and bloodless must be the
draining of this victim's life. Its energies were
needed as solvents and lubricants, to melt the seals
and oil the hinges of the dungeon door through
which Orcus must eventually pass if it was finally
decided to free him. Wood began to work now with
his most subtle arts, to extract the energies of
Chup's life without the use of material weapons.
Proceeding slowly and carefully, Wood ignored, or
at least he did not stop to savor, the reactions of the
victim whose mind must be made clear so he could
understand what was happening to him. The essential oil of despair must be added to those of fear and
pain. Chup, regaining his wits at last, strained at his
iron bonds, and looked up with a new and understanding horror at the man who was beginning to
kill him.

Wood had killed in ritual so often than now it
seemed no more important to him than the cracking
of an egg. While his voice chanted, and his hands
gestured, his mind held steady to the useful work-

ing image. Once more in imagination he had descended to the nethermost dungeon. Now he stood there like an artisan, a workman lubricating a lock, an intricate tremendous lock that held a massive door, a door securely sealed and barred, whose key had been put so far away that it had been forgotten. Another terrible ceremony would be needed for the recovery of that key, but that was for another day.

On the other side of the door, Wood knew, the monster moved (aye, he could feel and hear it through the door), the utter beast, a slouching, slimy and wall-bulging weight, that slid against the door, and turned within its tiny cell and padded on along the tiny circle it must walk. It was fully awakened now. He felt its foul breath issuing . . . enough. When he envisioned demons breathing, more than enough. The workman's image was the one that he must keep in mind. He must oil the unopenable hinges, and the lock, and make them ready to be used. Now, twist and squeeze the oily rag (whose name was Chup) to get the solvent and the lubricant. Probe deeply now into the lock and clear the sealing force from all the parts . . .

Incredibly, the workman's hand upon the door was seized, by something from the other side. Wood's hand went dead as ice. A numbing shock flew all along his arm. He tried to step back from the door, to pull away. When that effort failed he sought to tear his mind out of the image at once, terrible though the dangers were in doing so. But still his hand was held. He could only gape in horrified disbelief as the monster, having been somehow granted some kind of fingerhold within the lock, proceeded to make good use of it, applying his full strength.

The lock went smash at once, the crossbars on the door were splintering. The weight against the other side leaned harder and the bars broke off. Slowly, leisurely almost, the door swung on its hinges open-

ing . . . with an effort inspired by ultimate terror,
Wood broke away, returning to his body in the world
of men.

Charmian, still watching her husband's face intently, was the first person outside the wizards' ring
to understand that something was going hideously
wrong. She saw Chup's face change once more, a
new kind of calm replacing the understanding fear,
and she thought that he was on the point of death.
For mixed reasons, she felt a pang of disappoint-
ment, and was unconsciously drawing herself up to
express her feelings in some gesture when she saw
that which converted her movement into the start of
a retreat.

Suddenly she saw that Chup's right hand, showing not even a tremor, moving with deliberate sure-
ness, had pulled itself free of its restraint (had those
straps ever been iron, that now lay twisted like torn
cloth?) and was moving to take hold of the thicker
iron band across his chest. The hand found its grip,
and quivered once. With a ringing snap the chest-
band burst, sending a fragment of metal singing like
a missile past Charmian's head. Not that Chup's
actions had anything to do with her; his eyes, with
their new and terrible calm, were fixed on Wood.

Wood, his eyes meeting that gaze, stood frozen for
a long moment, his practiced hands for once contorted awkwardly. Similarly his two assistants were
transfixed, one with arms outthrust as if to ward off
a lunge by Chup, the other bent forward ludicrous-
ly, as if with stomach-ache. Every detail of the tab-
leau seemed in that moment to be carved of stone.

Then Wood's hands shot forward, fingers
clenched, thumbs pointing, aimed like some boy's
hands holding a strange and imaginary weapon in
play. Toward Chup's rising figure, garbed in the
rude, stained robe of a sacrifice, there leaped out
from Wood's hands a soundless scimitar-curve of
multicolored light. It flashed from the wizard across

nearly the entire space that separated him from Chup. But the last half-meter of space remained inviolate.

The counterblow Charmian could not see directly, only its effect. To her, watching in a timeless moment of terror, it seemed that Wood's face stayed where it was, a malignant frozen mask, while behind it and below it his head and body were shattered into bloodless clods and dust. Then the face disintegrated into flying dust. Simultaneously Wood's two aides were flung aside like rags. The blow that had struck the wizards went in a soundless shock through air and earth. Charmian fell to her knees. In the aftermath she heard the men of the army yelling and running away.

The body that had been Chup's stood tall and seemingly unscathed, turning to and fro to look and listen. Charmian saw that the camp a little distance off was full of tumbled tents and running men. Black-garbed wizards came running nearer, then turned and fled, or stood and trembled helplessly, when he who had been Chup looked at them. No trace of Wood was left, and the two who had been helping him were rolled-up rag-bundles on the ground. Charmian was the only living person within fifty meters of Chup's terrible eyes, and now they turned to her.

Still on her knees, she now stretched forth her arms. "Ardneh." Her voice was quavering, almost inaudible, even to herself. "Ardneh, mercy—a thousand thanks and mercies are your due, for having slain that man who held me as his slave."

The eyes that had been Chup's held her only a moment longer, then moved back to scan the turmoil in the camp. Suddenly a voice more terrible than Chup's boomed from the throat that had been his: "Hear me, humans, vermin of the earth! I, the Emperor Orcus, have come to reclaim my throne, and to put all the world beneath my feet. Know and believe this, and hold yourselves in readiness to

obey. Your fates depend upon how faithfully you
serve me in the battle soon to come against the West.
For now, farewell."

Only Charmian was near enough to see what happened next. The body that had been Chup's was
racked by a prolonged shuddering, making the departure of the possessing power effectively visible.
Suddenly it was once more her husbnad who stood
before her.

Chup drew a deep breath, like a man returning
from an underwater plunge. There was wonder in
his eyes, but not bewilderment; he had evidently
been conscious of all that happened while Orcus
used his body to escape.

Chup's gaze came to rest on Charmian. She gave a
low, choked cry, got to her feet and tried to flee, but
before she could take a step Chup's hard hand
clamped her arm.

"We are going to leave," said Chup in a quiet rasp.
"I think no one will try to stop thc Emperor Orcus as
he walks away."

"My own true Lord," said Charmian, with something like a sob. "I know what you must think of me; I
do not care, now that I see you whole and free again.

"Move out," he said, preoccupied with looking for
pursuit. Thousands of distant eyes were on him, but
no one in the shaken army of the East was offering to
come closer. "Try to raise an alarm and I will break
your spine before they get me."

Thus they walked away.

When Orcus first came fully awake within his
more-than-physical dungeon his first clear thought
was that someone or something was helping him,
reaching to give him unforced and willing aid. Powerful abilities besides his own were laboring to set
him free, dispersing the fogs and webs of enchantment that had kept him more than half asleep, letting into his cell a light of almost blinding clarity.
Never before had Orcus been given free and willing

help, and the motives of his helper now loomed as a mystery. But he had no time now for asking questions, no time for anything but the giant effort he must make to win his freedom.

The magical images in which Orcus saw the event were jumbled, not as clear as Wood's dungeon door and lock. But Orcus saw the way that he must take. The man who was being drained and used by Wood became for Orcus first a handgrip, a fragment of real life thrust near him in his prison of chaos. And then the human fragment became a lifeboat bobbing and tossing on a mad sea. Made able to think and move again by some unknown source of outside help, Orcus possessed the man and used him, poured his own demonic bulk into the little matrix of the human brain, and by this fulcrum levered his own titanic energies back into the world of men.

After that it was the work of a moment or two to release his borrowed body from its physical bonds, that he might more readily use it if he chose. It was only the work of another moment to strike Wood down. After that, a quick survey of the immediate situation, and the human body provided a convenient voice for the Demon-Emperor to use in announcing his return to the assembled human army of the East.

Even as he spoke, his thoughts and perceptions raced ahead. He felt some regret at slaying Wood so quickly. Age-long revenge on those who had betrayed him was desirable, and Wood must have been among them, as surely as the arch-traitor must have been Ominor. But meanwhile, Orcus saw and understood why Ominor had dared to think of bringing him back into the world. The danger from the West was presently very great. Without Orcus the East would not be strong enough to meet it. And if the West prevailed, the intriguers of the East would find that they had nothing to steal from one another.

At the heart of the danger from the West there

loomed a power new to Orcus; new and strange, and
stronger than any that he had ever faced before.
Whether the strength of this new enemy was greater
than his own he could not immediately determine,
but he had the impression that the force of this
enemy was still waxing. The enemy had a name,
Ardneh. The name was unhidden, arrogantly
revealed—make what magical use of it you like,
malign powers of the East. Ardneh glowed, in the
spectra of several energies, with deadly enmity for
Orcus and all his works. All these things Orcus perceived within moments after re-entering the world
of men, while still looking through the eyes of the
man who was to have been sacrificed.

With his chief enemy waxing stronger, there was
no point in delaying the struggle that must come.
Casting aside the man he had possessed, Orcus
mounted in a silent invisible rush into the upper air.
From there, he swept the great curve of earth with
his multitude of senses. He saw the dispositions of
the main armies of both East and West, and he saw
something more, that all but caused him to disre-
gard those armies. Some kilometers north of the
spot from which he had arisen, he sensed a series of
chambers under the ground, and a concentration of
life that moved and pulsed therein. Despite the distance, and the magical defenses that ringed it all
about, to Orcus the nature of the place was plain,
and the identity of the life within it. Above that place
the Demon-Emperor flew slowly, and then toward it
he went falling like an avalanche.

Inside one of the caves of Ardneh, Rolf saw the
lights go dim. At the same moment came a heighten-
ing in intensity of the ubiquitous hum of technological power, usually so low that he was doubtful of
hearing it at all.

"Ardneh?"

There was no immediate answer, no feeling of
Ardneh's presence.

Going toward the outer room where he had seen
Catherine working a few minutes before—it seemed
there were always more cables to be connected,
more devices unpacked or moved—Rolf met her
coming, wide-eyed, to look for him.

There was unconcealed fright in her voice. "Rolf,
it has gone dark outside. The sun is gone."

He felt his own heart lurch, but tried to appear
calm. "Not the sun. If it's dark, it must be something . . ."

Ardneh interrupted, speaking from above them
and seemingly from all around them, louder than
they had ever heard him before. "The days of the
decisive battle have begun. Orcus, emperor of demons, has found me and is attacking. Do not let the
darkness outside worry you. It is local, and is part of
my defense."

"Ardneh, what can we—"

"Go to Room Three at once, and stand by to re-
connect the generators there."

When they had been working for a little time in
the chamber that Ardneh had taught them to call
Room Three, he interrupted his detailed technical
orders to inform them: "I have repulsed the first
attack of Orcus. He will make further efforts, but our
struggle is not likely to be decided now until the
armies of men have come to join it. Meanwhile there
are more changes in equipment to be made."

During the remainder of the day Rolf and
Catherine were kept at work. Now and again the
earth shook around their armored, buried rooms.
The walls yielded a little and swayed with the moving of the earth, but were not crushed or broken.
Rolf discovered that another of the outer rooms had
been sealed off by heavy sliding doors.

Late in the day, Ardneh gradually ceased to issue
orders. The sense of his presence became remote,
while the demonic aura of his unimaginable opponent, that the humans had begun to sense, disap-

peared completely. Catherine and Rolf sat, waiting
and resting amid their tools.

After a while, Catherine asked: "What will you do,
Rolf, when the war is over?"

"Over?" From time to time he had enjoyed vague
thoughts of victory celebrations, and once or twice
he had meditated on some vengeance against the
East. But such things still seemed as far away as
ever.

Catherine added: "Ardneh has told us it will almost certainly be over very soon. Remember?"

"Of course." He tried to visualize what victory
would be like; the other possibility was hardly to be
contemplated. "I can't really remember what things
were like before the war; at least, not before the East
came to occupy us. I was only a child then."

"You were telling me yesterday about your family,
and how the seacoast looked near where you lived.
In the Broken Lands."

Rolf was silent for a time. "I can't see myself just
going back to farm the land my parents held. No, I'll
do something else. Some new work in technology,
maybe. I don't know where. Will you be with me
then? When all the curses of the East are dead?" He
hadn't meant to come out with the words so bluntly,
but now that they were out he had no wish to call
them back.

Catherine looked at him, and began to give her
answer with luminous eyes, and then her eyes
looked past him. Rolf spun round barely in time to
meet the soft-footed rush of the first wolf.

After struggling for a full day against Ardneh,
Orcus broke off the fight temporarily and withdrew
into the upper atmosphere meaning to recharge his
depleted energies while he restudied the situation.

During the struggle he had learned several things
about his opponent. For one thing, Ardneh was certainly formidable. For another, it was virtually cer-

tain that Ardneh would never pursue him. Orcus
was definitely the more mobile, while Ardneh
perhaps had an advantage in strength, as long as he
was content merely to defend the little plot of land
wherein his life was buried.

Brooding as he rested kilometers above that land,
Orcus pondered the inky cloud of Ardneh's defensive energies. To penetrate that concentrated block
would probably prove more than even the Emperor
of Demons could accomplish without help.

Lying atop the atmosphere, Orcus spread himself
thin as a blanket, absorbing energy from the sun and
from incoming cosmic particles. When he had re-
charged his strength somewhat he summoned up a
minor demon to be his messenger. This one he sent
to find Ominor, and convey to the man Orcus's blunt
orders. Ominor was to bring his human army north
with all possible speed, encircle Ardneh, and do all
that massed human strength could achieve in the
way of digging him out of his defenses. While this
effort was in progress, Orcus would renew his own
assault. The Western army might well try to inter-
vene, but it could not long sustain a pitched battle
against Ominor, and no other kind of battle could
now save Ardneh from destruction.

A crushing victory for the East was near. After it,
Orcus planned to enjoy agelong revenge against
John Ominor.

The first wolf had gone down with Catherine's
arrow through its body, but not before Rolf's left
forearm had been severely bitten. The two of them
were fleeing now, feet pounding in the darkened
corridors, behind them the howls of a pursuing
pack. The humans cried for help as they ran; Ardneh
closed doors against their pursuers were possible,
but evidently could do no more. And the doors that
could be closed were too few to effectively cut off
the chase, though they afforded a temporarily life-
saving delay.

"To the tunnel," Rolf gasped. It was the narrowest place that he could think of. "We may be able to hold them there."

On the narrow stone ledge beside the stream, with his back to daylight, he was ready with his sword for the first red-eyed howler's spring, and caught it on his point. Others came splashing in the stream beside him. Catherine hit one with a shaft, but before she could draw again a furry body had knocked her down.

Rolf threw himself into the water, his blade dividing fur and bone. Catherine fought with a knife drawn from her belt. Standing together in the bloodied water it seemed for a moment that they might hold . . .

Sunlight was darkened behind them. A bulk of fur that nearly filled the tunnel had entered it on all fours.

Rolf's swordblade had wedged in a wolf's skull and he strained desperately to wrench it free. Meanwhile the claws of the mountainous new beast were reaching for him from behind . . .

Not claws. The hand of an orange-furred giant closed round his ribs. He was lifted, swept backward, tossed into sunlight to land in mud and water with a great splash. He had just time to catch a breath before Catherine came flying to land almost in his arms. He pulled her head above water and she gasped for air.

Now, where was his sword—?

What seemed like long minutes were necessary to locate the weapon, stuck in the bottom mud. But it was not needed sooner. Seeing into the shadowed tunnel from sunlight was effectively impossible, but sounds came plainly out: wolf-howls that keened in agony, and what sounded like words, muttered in a basso voice. There came out broken lupine bodies, drifting. Rolf had his sword back in his hand before a single live wolf emerged at last, in a dead frantic yelping run. He cut at and missed the speeding form, and listened to the sounds of its flight diminish in the distance.

Now something else was stirring in the tunnel mouth. A giant's hand, covered with orange fur, and somewhere he had once seen the like before . . .

"Lord Draffut," Rolf choked out, and sat down on the stream's bank, with suddenly trembling knees. "We give you welcome."

Catherine marveled greatly, and her awe increased when Draffut laid hold gently of Rolf's mangled arm and raw, torn flesh became half-healed scar tissue at his touch.

"My healing powers are not what they once were," the Beast-Lord rumbled. "Yet what I can give to humans I still give."

"Lord Draffut, we thank you."

"Ardneh has called me, and I have listened." With his great hands he touched and began the healing of their smaller wounds as well. Then, with Catherine's two hands held in one of his, he paused, looking down into her eyes as an adult might regard an infant. "I sense another matter of pain, that has been visited upon you. The work of healing that has already been begun, also."

"We thank you again."

"No, you have begun it yourselves."

Rolf, feeling childlike in size and wisdom, exchanged looks with Catherine. "I do not understand."

"Rolf. Have you not now bound yourself to Catherine, so that her life is to you as your own, and more than your own?"

Rolf still looked at her. "I have."

"Catherine, are you so bound to Rolf?"

"I am bound."

"Then from this day let your bodies be as one; no curse of the East can have power to separate you any more, whatever harm may otherwise be done to you."

The Lord Draffut very shortly took his leave, saying that many humans a little to the south were in great need of him, and soon there would be even more. Ardneh's mental presence meanwhile came fitfully to Rolf, with information.

"We are to rest now," he announced. "Inside."

He and Catherine were asleep, limbs twined on a spread cloak, when Ardneh's next speech broke an hours-long silence. "Rolf. Catherine. Get up, gather weapons and food. It is time for you to leave me."

Still half-sleeping, they arose in silence and began to dress. Almost immediately Ardneh spoke again: "You are to bear my last message to Duncan, and through him to all the West."

Rolf came fully awake at last. "Last message?"

"The eastern army has arrived, and is encircling me. I will be destroyed in a matter of hours."

Catherine ceased packing food into a bag and turned stunned eyes to Rolf, who groped for words but could not speak. Ardneh continued: "After you have memorized the message, you will follow the passage on the right just outside this room. You will find a door newly opened, leading to a tunnel that will bring you beyond the Eastern army."

Rolf found his tongue. "Catherine can take your message out, Ardneh. I will stay on and fight with you. You still need help. And—and it cannot be hopeless yet! I can help you devise some new—"

"No." The imperturbable calm of Ardneh's voice only made the meaning of his words the more unreal. "The next full scale attack of Orcus will destroy me, and it is not many hours away. And both of you must carry my message. We must make sure that it gets through. I no longer have any other means of communication with Duncan. You must impress upon him the importance of my final message, which is this: he will soon face the choice of either saving his army by retreat, or taking a grave risk of its destruction by trying to save me. He must choose to save the men. They can and will fight again tomor-

row. I am finished now. I must serve as I was meant
to serve.''

"I . . . Ardneh, is there no other way?"

"You can no longer give me meaningful help in
any other way. I have given you your orders now. I
will repeat the message several times before you
leave me."

"You will not need to repeat the message, I understand it." Rolf exchanged helpless glances with
Catherine. "If those are the orders you insist upon,
we must obey them. But . . ."

Catherine broke in, shouting angrily at the ceiling. "Ardneh, it is not right for you to be so calm. No
human being could be so, in your place. With
human beings, there is always a chance. Duncan
and our men can beat theirs in a pitched battle, if
they must. I feel it!"

"No."

Rolf cried: "Ardneh, do not surrender!"

"I will not, but Orcus with Ominor's army will be
strong enough to overcome me. Now tell this to
Duncan also, and spread it throughout the West: in
the future, men must not make gods of finite beings
like myself."

"Gods," Rolf repeated vacantly. He had heard the
word before, but it seemed to have no connection
with what was happening now. "Ardneh, tell us
what to do if you are killed."

"Bear my messages to Duncan. Then live and fight
for your humanity. And tell the army not to look
back on its retreat. That is important too."

Rolf went on arguing and pleading for a time,
though Ardneh no longer answered. Then Catherine, tears standing in her eyes, was thrusting a
pack at him, and his sword, and was pulling him by
the arm. At first Rolf moved dazedly, allowing himself to be led like some stunned prisoner. But when
they had reached the new door and passed into the
outer tunnel Ardneh had mentioned, he put
Catherine gently behind him and took the lead.

The new passage was crude and narrow, rough-walled, so dark that they must grope their way. From somewhere behind came the sliding closing of a heavy door. Now Ardneh's presence was very nearly gone from Rolf's perception.

After a hundred meters or so, the passage widened; and shortly its walls were no longer rock, but hardened earth. Yet it continued to twist on a long subterranean course. At last the slope they walked began gradually to tend upward, and there came to them warmer air, with the subtle smells of vegetation.

Their eyes strained ahead for light, but there was none, not even the tenuous sky-glow of a cloudy night. "We must be still within the blackness," Rolf whispered softly.

The walls of the tunnel grew further apart, then abruptly fell away altogether. Rolf could not tell how Ardneh had arranged the opening, or prevented the enemy from getting into it. But there was no doubt that Ardneh's messengers had reached open air; Rolf felt a tuft of grass now brush against his leg.

Ardneh had said that the tunnel would bring them above ground behind the Eastern lines, outside the noose that Ominor had drawn around Ardneh's emplacement. Under Orcus's orders, the Eastern army had evidently dared to enter Ardneh's zone of darkness; Rolf and Catherine could now hear the mutter and murmur of a great number of men working some distance away, the crunching and scraping of innumerable digging tools. The noise came from somewhere behind them as they faced away from the tunnel mouth from which they had just emerged.

Reaching behind him to hold Catherine's left hand in his own, Rolf led on, away from the sounds of digging. The darkness at first remained absolute. Soon he paused; at a few score meters' distance there came the sound of men in a column tramping past. The marchers were led by a chanting wizard, who bore aloft a kind of witchlight that illuminated a few square meters of the land that Ardneh had interdicted from all light; at Rolf's distance, no more than a blurred blue spark was visible. After the wizard passed, came the sound of feet in route step, an occasional chink of tools or weapons, and a hushed fragment or two of Eastern talk. Weapons ready, Catherine and Rolf stood motionless until the spark had faded to invisibility and the column was out of earshot.

Moving on, they soon found the ground sloping downward again beneath their feet. Now Rolf put each foot forward with extra caution.

At last one of his feet found water.

"The river," Catherine whispered in his ear.

"It must be." But, he thought, the river wound around Ardneh, so to find it was little help in judging directions. Anyway, compass directions in themselves would be useless until he knew where Duncan was.

"Let us try to wade it," he whispered. If it came to swimming they might face the question of leaving their heavy metal weapons behind. Easing his way into the water, Rolf made sure to note immediately the direction of the current; if they should get to floundering and swimming in midstream, it wouldn't do to get turned around and come out unknowingly on the bank from which they had gone in.

Good fortune attended the crossing, however, through water nowhere more than waist deep. On the new bank, the grass was thicker, and the earth seemed flatter, less disturbed. When they had advanced a hundred meters beyond the riverbank, the sounds of tramping, working men were no longer audible. The normal summer sounds of bird and insect were absent too. Silence seemed complete.

Rolf, still leading, stopped so abruptly that Catherine stepped on his heel. Suddenly there had become visible to him the glimmering beginning of bright sunlight, a tentative vision caught first with one eye only, like something manufactured by the sight-starved nerves inside his head. But when they had moved forward a few more steps, there appeared a splintered, fragmented scene of daylit grass and sky.

Before emerging from Ardneh's night, Rolf called a halt to rest and wait for the setting of the sun. He and Catherine remained where they were until the dimming of the light ahead showed that natural darkness was falling. Then they moved out from under the mountain-sized shadow beneath which Ardneh hid; they had not gone a hundred meters under the open sky before a bird came drifting down on silent wings to greet them.

XI

World Without Ardneh

"We have messages for Duncan, from Ardneh," Rolf told the bird at once. "Can you guide us to him, quickly?"

"Whoo. It will take yoouu half the night to reach his camp. I had better bear your words."

"The army is still so far? Ardneh needs his help."

"They were closer this morning, before the day's fighting began. Tonight Duncan retreats. Some of us Feathered Folk were sent to watch for youuu."

Rolf drew a deep breath. "Yes, you had better bear Ardneh's words. We will follow as quickly as we can." Rolf repeated Ardneh's injunctions, word for word as closely as he was able. "And now, which way does Duncan's army lie?"

The bird rose briefly out of sight, then dropped back to earth and pointed with one wing. "There, only a little way, and youu will meet the ground patrol whoo cared for me through the day. I will tell them first that yoouu are here, then carry Ardneh's messages on."

With that the bird was gone. Rolf was relieved to make contact with the foot patrol of eight men after only another hundred meters' cautious advance. From them, he and Catherine soon learned that Duncan's efforts to break the Eastern ring round Ardneh's redoubt had been fierce but unsuccessful.

"I think you had better take us straight to Duncan," Rolf told the patrol's leader. "We can give him

more information than you are likely to gain,
stumbling about here without your bird."

The officer was opening his mouth to answer
when the night around them erupted with the clash
and yells of ambush. The clutch of sudden terror
was no less sharp for being an old acquaintance.
Rolf drew and crouched low, trying to see the enemy
outlined against the sky. Men rushed and struggled
around him, and for the moment he could not distinguish foe from unfamiliar friend, and he did not
strike.

Amid the grunting and shouting there came a
single high-pitched scream, from what direction he
could not be sure. He called out Catherine's name.
The only answer came from death, singing to his
right and left in invisible blades. Rolf threw himself
down, rolled away in the grass, and battle-noise
swept past him.

The pounding and scurrying of feet dwindled into
silence. Suddenly, inexplicably as could happen in
a night action, he found himself apparently alone.
Cautiously he rose into a crouch, probing the silent
night with all his senses. In the middle distance
faint moonlight shone on a crawling form that might
be Catherine's, half-hidden in tall grass. Rolf moved
in that direction, stepping slowly at first, then with
a short rush when the form seemed to waver and
vanish in the light of the deceptive moon.

At the spot where he thought the figure had been,
he called Catherine's name again, softly, several
times, but there came not so much as a rustle of
grass in response. He searched in a small circle, but
there was no trace of anyone.

Rolf realized that with every passing moment the
chance of finding her here grew more remote. If she
was still alive, she must be moving on ahead of him
toward Duncan, in the direction the patrol had
started to take before the ambush. In that direction
Rolf's duty also urged him. He took his bearings by

the stars and at last moved on alone. Somewhere off to his left, men brawled with steel again and then were silent. Rolf kept his weapon ready and held to his course.

Throughout the rest of the night he maintained a steady progress. Once he came upon a bird lying in the moonlight, dead since the day before most likely, the great wings broken and torn, probably by reptile claws, and the wide eyesockets emptied. Rolf could not tell if it was a bird he knew; it might have been Strijeef for all that he could tell.

At dawn Rolf could see, but not identify, groups of people in the distance, in several directions. He took cover; fortunately the grass here was tall enough to hide him as he crawled. Well behind him now, Ardneh's dome of darkness, impervious to sun, still bulked high against the clear sky. Rolf saw numbers of reptiles in the distance, but all appeared to be occupied with matters of more moment than his solitary passage. When a rise of ground shielded him from the distant people, he stood and walked again.

Near the middle of the morning he knew a great, heart-numbing shock as he came upon Catherine lying dead in bloody rags. But when he turned the body over he saw it was that of some long-haired Western boy of slender build. Quivering in all his limbs, Rolf had to sit down. But at once renewed hope began to grow. Perhaps she was somewhere just ahead of him, or close behind. They might find each other even before they reached the Western army.

Around noon Rolf had to make a long detour to get round a large Eastern foot patrol. He hoped Catherine had retained her waterbottle. Most of his own was gone by now. The sun beat down into tall windless grass. Only now and then came the ghost of a breeze, cooling his face.

Shortly after he got past the Eastern patrol Rolf came in sight of what he took to be Duncan's rear-

guard. In another hour of cautious pursuit he ha
gained enough ground to be sure; the long, thick,
twisting column of the retreat was plainly in sight
now, going up a gradual rise of land toward the
southwest. The retreat was still heading directly
away from Ardneh's shadow-dome, which was now
many kilometers distant across the tree-dotted sea
of grass.

When he came in hailing distance of the mounted men who brought up the army's rear, he was
assured that Duncan himself was only a short distance ahead. Alternately walking and trotting, moving up along the column, Rolf could see the special
bitter weariness of defeat in every face. It had been
defeat, but not disaster; the army was basically in-
tact. Men had retained their weapons, the wounded
were being borne efficiently along on animals and in
litters.

Duncan was riding alone, in battle-stained clothing, a little apart from his chief officers. When Rolf
came trotting at his stirrup, Duncan looked down,
at first with weary curiosity, then with delayed recognition and sudden new interest.

"Hail, Duncan." With a minimum of preamble,
Rolf passed on Ardneh's last admonitions, as nearly
word for word as he could manage to do.

"Yes, the bird came through with your message. I
thank you for all that you have done." A new thought
seemed to strike Duncan. "What happened to the
girl who was with you there?"

"I had hoped to find her here, sir."

Duncan looked sharply back over his shoulder,
made a little motion of his head, and a pair of men
among those riding a little distance to the rear
kicked their mounts into a faster pace that brought
them up to Duncan. These two men were well
dressed, and though armed they somehow did not
look like soldiers. A few words that Rolf did not
catch passed between them and Duncan, and then
they dismounted, let Duncan ride on ahead, and

came to walk beside Rolf, leading their animals. Meanwhile Duncan was engaged in some traveling discussion by some of his high officers.

The two well-dressed men introduced themselves to Rolf. "We are kinsmen of Catherine's," one explained, "and have come all the way from the Offshore Islands in search of her. At first we heard she was enslaved, and meant to try to ransom her; then were rejoiced to hear how she had escaped, with some Western soldiers, at some remote caravanserai. Now we hear that you are one of those soldiers, and that you have seen her lately. We entreat you, tell us whatever more you can."

Rolf nodded slowly, looking the men over. Both looked young, elegant, tough. "There is little enough to add." He turned away momentarily to look out over the surrounding grassy plain. Other stragglers like himself were still coming in, catching up with the army, but none of those in sight at the moment was a woman. Turning back, he asked: "To which one of you was she betrothed?"

"Neither," said one. They exchanged glances with each other. "We are both blood relatives. That one would not come."

Rolf felt his heart leap up; he could not convince himself that Catherine was really lying out there somewhere dead. He spoke then in a more friendly way to the Islanders, telling them what he could that might afford them some hope. He omitted the business of Charmian's curse.

The others in turn searched him carefully with their eyes, no doubt trying to ascertain what had been his exact relationship with their kinswoman. They had him repeat parts of his story—where and when he had seen her last, how was her general health. Then, after offering courteous thanks, they mounted again and dropped back toward the rear of the column.

Now far back in that direction, directly above the shadow-shroud of Ardneh's beseiged redoubt, there came a silken ripple in the empty sky. Rolf felt a faint tilting of the world with a sensation like the beginning of nausea. In the sky there was a slash of purple hanging—imperial color, color also of injury, pain, obscenity, agony, like tissue swollen with blood, like the first brushstroke of some evil artist who meant to paint over all the smiling day. Orcus, coming again to the attack, slowly manifesting himself above his stubborn enemy.

The sight made no immediate difference in the pace of the Western army's stoic march. Some officer—yes, it was an old friend of Rolf's, Thomas of the Broken Lands—riding beside Duncan, began vehementaly to push the suggestion that the army fall back on and attempt to hold the natural citadel of the Black Mountains.

Duncan shook his head briefly. "Not against such power as drove us from the field yesterday. You were there. With one hand, or so it seemed, the king-devil yonder in the air nullified all that my best wizards tried to do against him; and with the other hand, so to speak, he did the same for Ardneh, and wore him down. While with the sword—well, we tried. I will not throw my army away. As many of our men fell as of the East, and as they outnumber us to begin with, I see no profit in that game. As for the citadel, you took it once, when superior magic was on our side. Could they not take it back, when their king-demon leads them?"

The two Offshore men, who had dropped back, were spurring forward now, passing Rolf and Duncan.

Thomas was saying: "Then we'll split up into small bands again. We'll start the war over from the beginning, if need be."

Far in the rear a thread of dust was rising from what must be another column of Eastern troops, entering the base of the mountainous shadow with which Ardneh had covered himself. Above the shadow, and bulking just about as large, a cloud of imperial purple disfigured the sky. It drew the eye and sickened the stomach like the first sight of death. One could grow accustomed to the sight of death, though; never to this. Rolf was awed despite himself when he began to realize the full immensity of Orcus. Ardneh's shadow was now so far away it would have been out of sight over the horizon, but for the gentle saucer-shape of the plain between. And the formless, purplish thing in the air above Ardneh looked as big as an egg held at arms' length. No single being could be that huge, Rolf told himself; but so it was.

Duncan, nodding wearily, was saying something in reply to Thomas's last remark. Whatever was being said, Rolf did not hear it, because now he was looking far ahead and watching Catherine's kinsmen spurring faster and faster forward along the slow column of the weary army. And now there was a brown-haired girl-figure running to them. The men were reining their animals to a dusty halt, leaping to the ground, embracing her.

Now the column was falling behind Rolf as he ran, all the dusty silent faces of it turning, each to watch him briefly as he came abreast and drew ahead. Her arm was pointing off to the right of the line of march. Thence I found my way, she must be explaining to her kinsmen. And now at last her face turned in Rolf's direction, and now she too began to run.

They stopped an arm's length short of touching. "You are alive, alive," Catherine kept saying, over and over, with her face contorted as if in tearful anger. Then she and Rolf seized each other.

After a little he noticed that the two Offshore men were standing nearby. The joy of finding Catherine was still in their faces, but now they were looking at Rolf even more closely than before. He must have exchanged some words with them, but later he had no clear memory of what they were.

"Ardneh's shadow is gone," said someone walking in the column near them, looking back.

Another said: "And the demon is descending on him for the kill.

Orcus and Ardneh, who today dwelt together again in their own place of intense and private violence, spoke to each other with great freedom and intimacy now, so closely were they grappled on all the levels of energy, so entwined were they in all the dimensions of space that they could find. While each strained to end the other's life, no other creature could hear what passed between them, but between them understanding flowed.

Orcus said (though not in human words): "Now it is finally proven and acknowledged between us that I have become stronger than you. My army of human slaves digs into your roots, and all your forces weaken as I myself descend to quench your life. In a moment more my will must prevail over yours, and it is my will that you be as nothingness, as if you had never been."

And Ardneh (in the same inhuman way of speech) replied: "So be it. I am willing to reach the end of life, for today all my tasks are ended too."

Orcus would not be distracted. "Die."

"I die, and at the moment of my death let go the Change that I have held upon the world. It is my will that the nuclear energies flow again; that you, hell-bomb creature, be as you were when my change first came upon you."

Only in that moment did Orcus understand who Ardneh was and what Ardneh's death would mean. In that same moment Orcus reversed the trend of all his magics, of all the evil spells around the world that drew from him; only in this manner might he reverse the fate that Ardneh had prepared. As a man dragged to the edge of a precipice will throw away all his treasures and his weapons, to grab with every finger for some saving hold, so did the Demon-Emperor now abandon all the threads of Eastern wizadry, leaving them to tangle, break, and recoil as

they might. Now he bent all his energies to stay
Ardneh from the brink of doom, seeing, at last, that
the two of them were flying toward it bound together.

Now it was Ardneh who strained toward the brink
of extinction, bent on ending his own weakened life.
The momentum of the struggle tending in that direction was too great for Orcus to stop it now. Orcus
felt that his own reversed efforts were failing, and
knew such terror as he could know.

Twenty kilometers from where the struggle between Orcus and Ardneh was reaching its climax,
Charmian raised her head, startled by the sudden
disappearance of the dome of darkness. Chup, walking beside her, also turned his head to watch.

Since escaping from Ominor's camp, Chup had
been searching for Duncan's, but had had great difficulty keeping away from Eastern forces. Charmian
had stayed with him, not knowing if she dared try to
get away, or even if she wanted to. Would she be any
safer with Ominor himself? Now, it seemed, the Empire of the East belonged to one who was immune to
any human woman's charms.

In the distant sky, above where the dome of darkness had vanished, the cloud of silken purple sickness that was Orcus was contracting now, concentrating, falling, taking a shape like that of bird or
reptile to plunge majestically upon some victim.

Chup turned back sharply to say something to
Charmian, and froze when he caught sight of her
again.

Really she had felt nothing, no pain, no change. It
was only the expression on Chup's face that terrified her, waking the worst of her old nightmares,
making it come true by day.

"What are you goggling at?" she shrilled at him.
"What, what?" She heard her own voice crack most
strangely.

Chup would not say anything in answer. Neither would he stop staring.

She screamed croakingly at him again, and put her hand to her throat. When she saw it, her own hand, she let her aged crone's scream sound once more. And now, across her back, the crippling pain of stiffened age was undeniable. She cried out again, on and on and on. Only dimly was she aware that Chup was near her, reaching out.

To the Emperor John Ominor, astride his battle-stallion near the place where the border of darkness had been, and where now broad daylight fell on the massed thousands of his digging army, and on the hundred parts of Ardneh they had already up-rooted, there flew at this moment a minor demonic power who served him as bodyguard and personal sentry. It clamored a rapid warning: "Take flight! There is some trick, some trap! Orcus fights now for nothing but his own survival!"

Ominor's first thought was that this message it-self was a trick. But he could not see how taking flight might harm him. After the merest moment's delay, he pronounced a word that was unknown even to Wood, and that had remained unsaid for millenia. With the last syllable still on his lips the Emperor vanished from his saddle with a thun-derclap of sound that made even the war-stallion bolt. At the same moment, and with another crash of noise, Ominor reappeared upon a small hill some ten kilometers away. He staggered briefly with the sudden change from a riding to a standing posture, then found a solid footing in the grass. Looking around him at the place of temporary refuge that he had chosen in the moment before his flight, it seemed to him that he had chosen well. He was quite alone, and he could see plainly what was hap-pening around Ardneh, while being himself remote from any imaginable danger.

He peered back toward his army, and the ravaged plain in which its multitude was digging, and into which the purple form of Orcus had descended, to be absorbed like water in the earth. Nothing untoward seemed to be happening. But he would wait here a little to make sure. He could return to his army in a moment if necessary.

. . . suppose now that Ardneh were the winner. Assuming that most of the Eastern army could be salvaged, the Emperor Ominor (he did not yet concede that he had been deposed) saw certain advantages in such an outcome. A triumphant Orcus would be hard to cheat of his revenge, though Ominor still had a trick or two to play toward that end. At worst, whichever titanic power survived seemed likely to be weakened by the struggle. That Orcus and Ardneh should kill each other off was doubtless too much to wish for . . .

Thy wish is granted, said Ardneh softly in his mind.

Before John Ominor the world became pure light, the last light that he ever saw.

Ten kilometers farther from Ardneh and Orcus than Ominor had been, in the moment of the acid light that etched and ate the world, Rolf thought: Ardneh warned us not to look back; he must have meant literally that.

The light from behind them threw their long shadows ahead, shadows that were dark even in the teeth of the lowering sun. To keep Catherine's eyes turned forward, away from that terrible light, Rolf slid his arm around her neck. A thousand faces ahead of him were turning, to squint with astonishment and pain into the glare, then turning away again to shield their eyes. Within the distance of a few steps the army had shuffled to a halt.

On the exposed skin on the backs of Rolf's arms and legs, the heat grew swiftly to the point of pain, and then as swiftly dwindled. At the same time the

great light dimmed, leaving mere daylight that
seemed like darkness by comparison. Now, where
Ardneh's darkness had once been, and Orcus's sickening glow, a mighty fireball was crumbling in
upon itself like some vast ember, becoming a sphere
of brown, scorched smoke.

And now came the swiftest shockwave of the
blast, racing through the earth, rolling beneath
Rolf's feet and Catherine's. The earth smote up at
them as if in anger, and the long column of the army
staggered on its thousands of legs. Rolf saw grass
dancing, in a new, windless way. Then came the
soundwave with its deafening shock, and after that
a blast of wind that knocked the army down. Sterile
wind, cleaned and burned free of all energies of life,
but howling like a demon anyway, and hurling dirt
clouds like an elemental.

Scarcely were people able to stand up before the
wind hit them from the opposite direction and
knocked them down again. An avalanche of air was
rushing back toward the blasted center where now
around and below the crumpling fireball an airy
mountain of smoke and powdered earth began to
bloom. In all this furious movement there was no
smallest sign of life.

Now in Rolf's mind there was nothing left of
Ardneh, except in memory. Nor could he detect the
psychic weight of Orcus any longer. Above the place
where they had struggled, the mountainous column
of smoke and dust turned ever blacker as it rose
rapidly into the sky, curling and roiling into a mush-
room at its peak. From every quarter inrushing
winds bore tribute of more dust to build the pyre of
Ardneh and Orcus higher still toward the upper
air.

The army of the West was on its feet again, watching, in stunned silence. Finally Duncan, with some
difficulty controlling his frightened mount, began
talking out loud to himself: "Ominor's army. There,
and then gone. Like that. And the Demon-Emperor,

too. I'm magician enough to feel the certainty of that death. Annihilation. And Ardneh. Ardneh. Gone.''

The roar of the explosion seemed to persist, though now it was more in the mind and ringing ears than in the air. Kilometers away across the prairie, small scattered groups of refugees were coming into view, looking like ants beneath the titanic blast-cloud. Staggering, walking or running without evidence of purpose, human figures were moving like maddened insects across the scorched and wasted land.

Nearby, a human voice let out a roar. Rising in his stirrups, Duncan marveled: "Is that what's left of Ominor's reserve—? Why no, sweet demons! *Is that all that remains of the army of the East?*''

He wheeled his mount, and began to call out orders to his captains. Up and down the column, men and women came to life, and began to change the army's posture from retreat into a halt for rest and food, and preparation for new action soon.

Ever and again the people of the army paused in their work to watch the awesome cloud. At the height it had now attained, beyond that of any mountain ever seen, a wind was beginning to tear it away toward the desolate north. The ant-like Eastern survivors, or some of them at least, were moving closer across the plain, unknowing or uncaring that they approached the army of the West. Duncan ordered out squads of cavalry, to seek out any enemy units large or coherent enough to pose a possible threat. Among the stragglers coming in on one flank was a tall figure that Rolf thought he recognized; he began to walk toward it, Catherine coming with him.

Behind them, Duncan was shouting exultantly: "Wizards, will you read me your grim portents now? All your worst have been fulfilled today, and yet we stand in triumph! The East lies broken-backed before us, and ere autumn turns to winter we will be in their capital!''

"Chup!" Rolf reached to grip the tall man by the hand. "I see you were again too tough to die!"

Chup looked back at him strangely at first, not saying anything.

Rolf nodded to a slight, muffled figure that he had gradually become aware of standing in attendance at Chup's side. It appeared to be a female servant, burdened with a few bits of baggage, and wrapped in a blanket that concealed even her face. "Who's this?" he asked.

Catherine, bolder here than when she had last faced Chup, was moved to demand of him: "Is she some prize you've won at war? Did you not give up holding slaves when you joined the West?"

"A prize, maybe," said Chup. "But not of war." Unmoved, unreadable, he looked at Rolf and Catherine in turn. The crack of a smile appeared in his face, a new crevice in old rock. "This is my wife."

Rolf stared. Two strands of golden hair escaped the dingy blanket where it was drawn close around the figure's face.

"Oh, I'll answer for her behavior now. She has been . . . persuaded, as I once was, to join the West. When I've had a chance to explain the situation to a court, I doubt they'll want to visit any further punishment upon her. What has happened seems too . . . fitting . . . as it stands."

Behind them, in a group of the army's leaders, Gray's voice was orating: "Good Prince, if there is anything impossible to men, it is going back to what has once been changed. True, the Old World energies of nuclear power are once more with us, like outlandish demons that only technologists can control. But the energies of magic remain in force, still much stronger than they were in the days of Ardneh's origin. The world we live in from this day hence is a blend of Old and New, and so is doubly new. True, most of the evil spells that were in force yesterday are now nullified as a consequence of the defeat of Orcus. Others have been reversed . . ."

"It seems," Chup was saying, "that a certain evil
spell that this one laid upon a former serving-maid
was, like many another curse, turned back upon its
maker when the great demon fell. My lady here will
quickly turn into a hag, unless she receives the
proper treatment once or twice a day." Again Chup
smiled. "Before entering this camp I encountered
and questioned a certain pudgy wizard that I know.
I am informed by magical authority that no man's
stroking but my own is going to preserve my lady's
comeliness. Doubtless because I am the only man in
East or West who has ever thought or felt any more
for her than . . . well."

Chup suddenly put out a hand, to stroke the
cheek inside the blanket. And Catherine, watching,
was startled by the movement's gentleness.

FRED SABERHAGEN

Fred Saberhagen needs very little introduction these days. His most famous creations—the awesome Berserkers—are known to SF readers around the world. He's reached the bestseller lists several times, most recently with his "Book of Swords" series, and his novels span the territory from hard science fiction to high fantasy. Quite understandably, Saberhagen's been labeled one of the best writers in the business.

These fine novels by Saberhagen are available from Baen Books:

PYRAMIDS
A fascinating new twist on the time-travel novel, introducing a great new series hero: Pilgrim, the Flying Dutchman of Time, whose only hope for returning home lies in subtly altering the history of our own timeline to more closely reflect his own. Fortunately for us, Pilgrim's timeline is a rather more pleasant one than ours, and so the changes are—or at least are supposed to be—for the better. Learn why the curse of the Pharaoh Khufu (builder of the Great Pyramid) had a special reality, in *Pyramids*. "Saberhagen's light, imaginative and enjoyable adventures speed along twisting paths to a climax that is even more surprising than the rest of the book." —*Publishers Weekly*

AFTER THE FACT
This is the second novel featuring the great new series hero, Pilgrim—the Lost Traveller adrift in time and dimensionality. His current project: to rescue Abraham Lincoln from assassination, AFTER THE FACT!

THE FRANKENSTEIN PAPERS
At last—the truth about the sinister Dr. Frankenstein and his monster with a heart of gold, based on a history written by the monster himself! Find out what happened when the mad Doctor brought his creation to life, and why the monster has no scars.

THE "EMPIRE OF THE EAST" SERIES
THE BROKEN LANDS, Book I
A masterful blend of high technology and high sorcery; a unique adventure in a world on the brink of ultimate change; a world were magic rules—and science struggles to live again! *"Empire of the East* is one of the best science fiction fantasy epics—Saberhagen can be justly proud. Highly recommended."—*Science Fiction Review*. "A fine mix of fantasy and science fiction, action and speculation."—Roger Zelazny

THE BLACK MOUNTAINS, Book II
East meets West in bloody conflict on a world where magic rules, but technology is revolting! *"Empire of the East* is the work of a master!"—*Magazine of Fantasy and Science Fiction*

ARDNEH'S WORLD, Book III
The gripping climax of the "Empire of the East" series. "Ranks favorably with Tolkien. Exceptional in sheer unbridled zest and imaginative sweep." —*School Library Journal*

* * *

THE GOLDEN PEOPLE
Genetically perfect, super-human children are created by a dedicated scientist for the betterment of Mankind. As the children mature, however, they begin to wonder if Man *should* survive . . .

LOVE CONQUERS ALL
In a future where childbirth is outlawed and promiscuity required, one woman dares fight the system for the right to bear children.

MY BEST

Saberhagen presents his personal best, in *My Best*. One sure to please lovers of "hard" science fiction as well as high fantasy.

OCTAGON

Players scattered across the continent are engaged in a game called "Starweb." Each player has certain attributes, and can ally with or attack any of the others. But one player seems to have confused the reality of the world: a player with the attributes of machinelike precision and mechanical ruthlessness. His name is Octagon, and he's out for blood.

You can order all of Fred Saberhagen's books with this order form. Check your choices and send the combined cover price/s to: Baen Books, Dept. BA, 260 Fifth Avenue, New York, New York 10001.

PYRAMIDS • 320 pp. •
65609-0 • $3.50   _____
AFTER THE FACT • 320 pp. •
65391-1 • $3.95   _____
THE FRANKENSTEIN PAPERS •
288 pp. • 65550-7 • $3.50   _____
THE BROKEN LANDS • 224 pp. •
65380-6 • $2.95   _____
THE BLACK MOUNTAINS • 192 pp.
• 65390-3 • $2.75   _____
ARDNEH'S WORLD, Book III •
192 pp. • 65404-7 • $2.75   _____
THE GOLDEN PEOPLE • 272 pp. •
55904-4 • $3.50   _____
LOVE CONQUERS ALL • 288 pp. •
55953-2 • $2.95   _____
MY BEST • 320 pp. • 65645-7 •
$2.95   _____
OCTAGON • 288 pp. •
65353-9 • $2.95   _____

DAHUT, Book III
Dahut is the daughter of the King, Gratillonius, and her story is one of mythic power . . . and ancient evil. The senile gods of Ys have decreed that Dahut must become a Queen of the Christ-cursed city of Ys while her father still lives.   65371-7 $3.95

THE DOG AND THE WOLF, Book IV
Gratillonius, the once and future King, strives first to save the surviving remnant of the Ysans from utter destruction, and then to save civilization itself as barbarian night extinguishes the last flickers of the light that once was Rome!   65391-1 $4.50

ANDERSON, POUL
THE BROKEN SWORD
Come with us now to 11th-century Scandinavia, when Christianity is beginning to replace the old religon, but the Old Gods still have power, and men are still oppressed by the folk of the Faerie.

65382-2 $2.95

ASIRE, NANCY
TWILIGHT'S KINGDOMS
For centuries, two nearly-immortal races—the Krotahnya, followers of Light, and the Leishoranya, servants of Darkness—have been at war, struggling for final control of a world that belongs to neither. "The novel-length debut of an important new talent . . . I enthusiastically recommend it."—C.J. Cherryh
65362-8 $3.50

BROWN, MARY
THE UNLIKELY ONES
Thing is a young girl who hides behind a mask; her companions include a crow, a toad, a goldfish, and a kitten. Only the Dragon of the Black Mountain can restore them to health and happiness—but the questers must total seven to have a chance of success. "An imaginative and charming book."—*USA Today*. "You've got a winner here . . ."—Anne McCaffrey.

65361-X $3.95

DAVIDSON, AVRAM and DAVIS, GRANIA
MARCO POLO AND THE SLEEPING BEAUTY
Held by bonds of gracious but involuntary servitude in the court of Kublai Khan for ten years, the Polos—Marco, his father Niccolo, and his uncle Maffeo—want to go home. But first they must complete one simple task: bring the Khan the secret of immortality!

65372-5 $3.50

EMERY, CLAYTON
TALES OF ROBIN HOOD
Deep within Sherwood Forest, Robin Hood and his band have founded an entire community, but they must be always alert against those who would destroy them: Sir Guy de Gisborne, Maid Marion's ex-fiance and Robin's sworn enemy; the sorceress Taragal, who summons a demon boar to attack them; and even King Richard the Lion-Hearted, who orders Robin and his men to come and serve his will in London. And who is the false Hood whose men rape, pillage and burn in Robin's name?

65397-0 $3.50

AB HUGH, DAFYDD
HEROING
A down-on-her-luck female adventurer, a would-be
boy hero, and a world-weary priest looking for new
faith are comrades on a quest for the World's Dream.
65344-X $3.50

HEROES IN HELL

created by Janet Morris

The greatest heroes of history meet the greatest names
of science fiction—and each other!—in the greatest
meganovel of them all! (Consult "The Whole Baen
Catalog" for the complete listing of HEROES IN
HELL.)

MORRIS, JANET & GREGORY BENFORD,
C.J. CHERRYH, ROBERT SILVERBERG, more!
ANGELS IN HELL (Vol. VII)
Gilgamesh returns for blood; Marilyn Monroe kisses
the Devil; Stalin rewrites the Bible; and Altos, the
unfallen Angel, drops in on Napoleon and Marie
with good news: Marie will be elevated to heaven,
no strings attached! Such a deal! (So why is Napoleon
crying?)   65360-1 $3.50

MORRIS, JANET, & LYNN ABBEY, NANCY ASIRE,
C. J. CHERRYH, DAVID DRAKE, BILL KERBY,
CHRIS MORRIS, more.
MASTERS IN HELL (Vol. VIII)
Feel the heat as the newest installment of the
infernally popular HEROES IN HELL® series roars its
way into your heart! This is Hell—where you'll find

Sir Francis Burton, Copernicus, Lee Harvey Oswald, J. Edgar Hoover, Napoleon, Andropov, and other masters and would-be masters of their fate.

65379-2 $3.50

REAVES, MICHAEL
THE BURNING REALM

A gripping chronicle of the struggle between human magicians and the very *in*human Chthons with their demon masters. All want total control over the whirling fragments of what once was Earth, before the Necromancer unleashed the cataclysm that tore the world apart. "A fast-paced blend of fantasy, martial arts, and unforgettable landscapes."—Barbara Hambly

65386-5 $3.50

EMPIRE OF THE EAST
by Fred Saberhagen

THE BROKEN LANDS, Book I

A masterful blend of high technology and high sorcery; a unique adventure in a world on the brink of ultimate change; a world where magic rules—and science struggles to live again! "The work of a master." —*The Magazine of Fantasy & Science Fiction*

65380-6 $2.95

THE BLACK MOUNTAINS, Book II
East meets West in bloody conflict on a world where
magic rules, but technology is revolting! "A fine mix
of fantasy and science fiction, action and speculation."
—Roger Zelazny   65390-3 $2.75

ARDNEH'S WORLD, Book III
The gripping climax of the "Empire of the East"
series. "Ranks favorably with Tolkien. Exceptional
in sheer unbridled zest and imaginative sweep."
—*School Library Journal*   65404-7 $2.95

SPRINGER, NANCY
***CHANCE—AND OTHER GESTURES OF THE HAND
OF FATE***
Chance is a low-born forester who falls in love with
the lovely Princess Halimeda—but the story begins
when Halimeda's brother discovers Chance's feelings
toward the Princess. It's a story of power and jealousy,
taking place in the mysterious Wirral forest, whose
inhabitants are not at all human . . .

                                               65337-7 $3.50

THE HEX WITCH OF SELDOM (hardcover)
The King, the Sorceress, the Trickster, the Virgin,
the Priest . . . together they form the Circle of Twelve,
the primal human archetypes whose powers are
manifest in us all. Young Bobbi Yandro, can speak
with them at will—and when she becomes the
mistress of a horse who is more than a horse, events
sweep her into the very hands of the Twelve . . .

                                               65389-X $15.95